KU-637-737

Lucy Monroe started reading at age four. After she'd gone through the children's books at home, her mother caught her reading adult novels pilfered from the higher shelves on the book case...alas, it was nine years before she got her hands on a Mills & Boon® romance her older sister had brought home. She loves to create the strong alpha males and independent women that people Mills & Boon® books. When she's not immersed in a romance novel (whether reading or writing it) she enjoys travel with her family, having tea with the neighbours, gardening and visits from her numerous nieces and nephews. Lucy loves to hear from readers: email Lucymonroe@Lucymonroe.com or visit www.LucyMonroe.com

THE GREEK MILLIONAIRES' SEDUCTION: THE GREEK'S INNOCENT VIRGIN

Lucy Monroe

All the characters in this book have no existence outside the imagination of the author, and have no relation whatsoever to anyone bearing the same name or names. They are not even distantly inspired by any individual known or unknown to the author, and all the incidents are pure invention.

All Rights Reserved including the right of reproduction in whole or in part in any form. This edition is published by arrangement with Harlequin Enterprises II BV/S.à.r.l. The text of this publication or any part thereof may not be reproduced or transmitted in any form or by any means, electronic or mechanical, including photocopying, recording, storage in an information retrieval system, or otherwise, without the written permission of the publisher.

® and TM are trademarks owned and used by the trademark owner and/or its licensee. Trademarks marked with ® are registered with the United Kingdom Patent Office and/or the Office for Harmonisation in the Internal Market and in other countries.

First published in Great Britain 2005
Large Print edition 2010
Harlequin Mills & Boon Limited,
Eton House, 18-24 Paradise Road, Richmond, Surrey TW9 1SR

© Lucy Monroe 2005

ISBN: 978 0 263 21653 0

20226274

MORAY COUNCIL
LIBRARIES &
INFORMATION SERVICES
F

Harlequin Mills & Boon policy is to use papers that are natural, renewable and recyclable products and made from wood grown in sustainable forests. The logging and manufacturing process conform to the legal environmental regulations of the country of origin.

Printed in Great Britain
by Clays Ltd, St Ives plc

Hot-blooded, passionate men
who have everything—except brides...

MEDITERRANEAN MEN

The all-new Mediterranean Men
large-print collection gives you
top stories from your
favourite glitzy Modern collections
in easier-to-read print.

6 addictive large-print volumes

The Greek Millionaires' Seduction:
The Greek's Innocent Virgin
by Lucy Monroe

The Greek Tycoon's Takeover:
At the Greek Boss's Bidding
by Jane Porter

The Greeks' Bought Brides:
Bought for the Greek's Bed
by Julia James

The Italian Boss's Passion:
The Ranieri Bride
by Michelle Reid

The Italian's Summer Seduction:
The Italian's Price
by Diana Hamilton

The Italian's Baby Bargain:
The Italian's Wedding Ultimatum
by Kim Lawrence

CHAPTER ONE

RACHEL LONG felt curiously numb as she walked away from her mother's graveside, the scent of damp earth filling the hot Greek air.

Andrea Demakis had died at the age of forty-five and Rachel felt nothing. No outrage a life should be cut so short, no pain in the loss of a parent, no fear for the future.

She simply felt nothing at all.

Not even relief. The emotional turmoil her mother had visited on those around her was no longer Rachel's personal sword of Damocles, hovering above her and ready to shred her life again. And yet, she experienced no sense of liberation at the knowledge, merely emotional numbness in the face of the finality of death.

Her feet moved without her directing them,

carrying her away from the final statement of a life that had been lived with only one goal, self-gratification.

The service was long over and the other mourners had gone. All but one. Sebastian Kouros stood in the absolute stillness of extreme grief beside his great-uncle's grave. He had thrown the first handful of dirt onto the coffin, his steel gray gaze stoic, his big body rigid beneath the unrelenting Greek sun.

She stopped beside him, unsure what to say.

Or indeed if she should say anything at all.

His family had despised her mother and that contempt had glimmered in more than one pair of eyes when they had settled upon her today. No matter how many times she got the look that said *no doubt she'd been cut from the same cloth as her hedonistic mother,* it hurt. Only Sebastian had never allowed his obvious dislike of Andrea Demakis to impact the way he treated her daughter. He had always been kind to Rachel, gentle toward her shyness and even protective.

He had been the one to convince his great-uncle to pay for Rachel's university education, but would Sebastian's tolerance continue in the face of his beloved uncle's death?

After all, everyone knew why the old man was dead.

He'd married the wrong woman and not only had he lived to regret it, he'd died because of it.

The truth was, he could have died on any of numerous occasions over the past six years when Andrea had teased him into attempting physical feats better left to men half his age. Only he hadn't. He had died in a car accident, driving under the influence of alcohol and too much tension after yet another horrific argument with Andrea.

He'd caught his young wife in bed with another man…again.

They had fought in front of witnesses and then left the party. Rachel had learned her mother had only been in the car because when she'd refused at first to leave with him, Matthias had threatened to cut her off without a penny and divorce her. Motivated by self-interest when shame would have never swayed her, Andrea had gone with him.

And they had both died.

So, what could Rachel say to the grieving man beside her?

There were no words to undo the pain of the last six years, pain that had culminated in him losing the man who had stood in his father's stead since he was a young boy. Nevertheless, the compulsion to try could not be ignored.

She reached for his hand, hers trembling. "Sebastian?"

Sebastian Kouros felt the small fingers touch his, heard the tentative word quietly spoken and fought the urge to turn on Andrea Demakis's daughter with all the rage he wanted to vent against a dead woman.

"What is it *pethi mou?*" The endearment slipped out much too naturally when he was feeling in no way tender toward her, but she *was* little—barely five feet, five inches to his six-foot-four and he had followed his great-uncle's example, calling her by the endearment since first meeting Rachel.

"You're going to miss him." Her soft voice touched a place inside he could not afford to be stirred and maintain the precarious hold he had on his composure. "I'm sorry."

He looked down at her, but all he saw was chestnut brown hair pulled into a conservative French twist. Her face was averted.

"I also."

Moss green eyes came around to meet his own. "He should never have married Andrea."

"But the marriage changed your life, did it not?"

Her pale features flushed, but she nodded. "For the better. I can't deny it."

"And yet you chose to accept employment in the States, only returning to Greece for a few short weeks out of the year."

"I did not fit into their lifestyle."

"Did you try?"

Her eyes widened at his cold tone, their green depths darkening in confusion. "I didn't want to. I never liked living amid the chaos of Andrea's hectic social life."

"Had you no thought of trying to mitigate the effects of *your* mother's selfish nature on the life of a man who had done so much for you?"

She stepped away from him, removing her hand from his as if burned. "You cannot live another person's life for them."

"Indeed?" Part of him knew what she said was right.

He had been unable to stop his great-uncle from making the disastrous marriage, but the deep well of pain inside him denied a totally logical view of the old man's death.

"You profited by the marriage. The least you could have done was to at least try to curb Andrea's destructive behavior."

"I *couldn't* have done anything." Her words were firm, but her face was set in guilty lines and he knew she too wondered if she could have changed the steady downward spiral Andrea had made of Matthias's life. "I couldn't," she repeated.

"Perhaps in this, you also had no desire to try…" His voice trailed off on the subtle accusation and she flinched.

"I gave up trying to impact Andrea's lifestyle a long time ago." Rachel's voice reverberated with emotional hurt he could not ignore and he had a totally inappropriate urge to kiss the bow-shaped lips set in such an unhappy line until they were soft and glistening.

Until her eyes reflected sweet passion instead of a past filled with secret sorrows.

Damn it. There should be no room with the pain gripping his insides for this inexplicable desire.

It was the same appalling need that assailed him every time he came within ten feet of the beautiful, but reserved woman. His Greek mind could not reconcile wanting Rachel with the disdain he had felt for her mother.

By rights, he should despise Rachel as much as he had the selfish, ruthless woman who had given birth to her.

Rachel entered the masculine study with trepidation.

It had been Matthias Demakis's domain, the

only room in the large Mediterranean villa on the privately owned Greek island that her mother had not redecorated. In the past, this room with its rich red upholstered chairs and dark wood paneling had been the setting for two of her happiest moments: the evening Matthias had told her she no longer had to attend her mother's parties despite Andrea's demands and the day the old man had told her he was sending her to university in America.

However, today promised no joy.

She had been called down to attend the reading of the wills. Since her conversation at the graveside with Sebastian the day before, she'd spent most of her time in her room. The Kouros and Demakis families were in residence and she had no desire to make herself a whipping boy for their grief and entirely righteous anger. Justified it might be, but she was not the one who had destroyed Matthias Demakis's life.

Sebastian's accusation that she should have tried to stem Andrea's devastating behavior had been ludicrous, but she'd had no desire to laugh.

He held her responsible for her mother's sins and that hurt more than she wanted to contemplate.

The one man in all the world she'd ever wanted physically, the only man she'd trusted enough to swim with or talk to alone on a balcony of the old villa late at night, hated her. Her mother's death had not resulted in personal anguish, but the knowledge Sebastian was forever out of her reach did.

She'd paid the price for being Andrea's daughter for twenty-three years. Must she keep paying it, even now that the other woman was dead?

"Miss Long, won't you take a seat?" The white haired lawyer had been on Matthias's retainer for decades, but still maintained an aura of vitality she couldn't help but admire.

As Matthias had…before he'd married a woman more than twenty-five years his junior.

Rachel tried not to make eye contact with anyone else as she made for a small ottoman in the back of the room set against a bookcase. She sat down, smoothing her hands nervously over the oyster white loose trousers covering her legs.

The current trend of tight clothes that showed strips of skin had not made its way into her closet despite the fact she lived in Skin Central— Southern California.

Phillippa Kouros, Sebastian's mother and Matthias's niece, came into the room to take a seat beside her son. Although the powerful man's back was to her, Rachel had no problem reading his body language as he solicitously cared for his mother and then turned to the lawyer and gave him permission to begin.

Andrea's will held few unexpected details. She'd left all her worldly goods to her husband, except in the event he preceded her in death, then her possessions were to pass on to Rachel. The sequence of bequeathals did not surprise her. Andrea would never have expected Matthias to outlive her and had no doubt made the stipulation as some manipulative attempt at making him believe she valued him even above her daughter.

However, Matthias Demakis's last will and testament was somewhat surprising. Although he had left a few things of sentimental value to his family members and Rachel, the bulk of his estate had been passed down to Sebastian Kouros, including the villa.

He had made no provision at all for his younger wife, nor had he left instructions for Sebastian to care for the widow. Knowing how his family had felt about Andrea, that omission was telling to Rachel's way of thinking. Evidently, Matthias had grown completely disenchanted with his wife's peccadilloes and scandalous behavior.

The white-haired lawyer set the document down after he had finished reading it and fixed his blue gaze on Rachel, which effectively brought the attention of the other occupants of the room as well.

Rachel squirmed inside at the stares directed her way.

"The coroner was unable to determine which of the occupants of the car died first." The lawyer's gaze shifted to Sebastian. "However, I'm sure the family will not dispute you taking possession of your mother's personal belongings."

Sebastian's head shook in a slight negative.

Rachel felt nothing, certainly no joy in possessing anything resulting from her mother's misbegotten lifestyle. The one thing she would have gladly received from Andrea, the other woman had taken to the grave with her.

The identity of Rachel's father—a piece of information her mother had refused to part with throughout Rachel's life.

Sebastian looked up at the sound of a knock on the study door. It was open, but Rachel did not come in. She stood framed in the opening, her face cast in shadow by the light coming in from the hallway so he could not see her expression.

He didn't like that and he waved her inside impatiently, having expected this visit, but not pleased his cynicism had been proven right. As much as he knew she was Andrea's daughter, he'd always wanted to believe she didn't share her mother's avarice.

"Come in. You don't have to stand in the hall."

She stepped forward, entering the room like a wary doe in the hunter's sights. "I didn't want to intrude."

"If I needed privacy, the door would be shut."

"Of course." She took a deep breath, avoiding direct eye contact, her hands fisted at her sides. "Do you have a moment? I have some things I need to discuss with you."

He nodded toward one of the red leather chairs he and his mother had occupied when the wills were read earlier. "Have a seat. I know what you want to talk about and I'm sure we can come to an amicable arrangement."

Rachel had taken the news she'd inherited virtually nothing with too much calm acceptance earlier that day. Any offspring of the scheming Andrea would have expected a large settlement on the death of her wealthy stepfather. Rachel had to have been seriously disappointed.

The small set of books on Hellenic culture Matthias had bequeathed to her had been nothing more than a sentimental nod to the evenings he had spent discussing Greek history with his stepdaughter. Even if she sold them, they would net her only a few thousand dollars.

Sebastian saw no reason to refuse Rachel a

settlement…in exchange for a vow of silence on her mother's years as Matthias Demakis's wife. He had no desire to read sleazy stories in the gutter press given credence by paid for interviews with Andrea Demakis's daughter.

Rachel slid into the red chair, its oversize winged back giving her the appearance of a child. Or perhaps a fairy queen. Children did not have curves that haunted men's dreams and sparked their libidos. He knew Rachel did, even if the white pants and top she currently wore did nothing to reveal the hourglass figure he'd seen on the few occasions she'd swum with him in his great-uncle's pool.

She was as unassuming and conventional as her mother had been flamboyant and morally corrupt. At least on the surface.

How much of that innocence was real?

Considering the discussion they were about to have, he would have to assume a very small part.

"I shouldn't be surprised you expected me." A smile briefly lifted the corners of Rachel's mouth. "You've always seen things others tend to ignore."

"Certainly more than my uncle did when he looked at your mother."

An emotionless mask descended over Rachel's porcelain features, all vestiges of her smile dissipating like mist under a warm sun. "No doubt."

"And I suppose this is what you wish to discuss with me?" The fact Matthias Demakis had finally wised up to his grasping, faithless wife leaving neither her, nor her daughter anything of real value in his will.

"In a way, yes." She sat up straight in the chair and then shifted her legs so that one crossed over the other. "I need to return to my job fairly soon."

"Yes?"

"And there are my mother's things to be gone through."

"Did you want to delegate that task to the servants?"

"No." Her mouth pursed as if in distaste at the thought. "That wouldn't be right, but I need to know what you want me to do with them."

"Surely that is a decision you must make."

"I'd considered donating her clothes and jewelry to charity, but then I realized there was the possibility Matthias had given her family heirloom pieces. I'm sure you wouldn't want them to go to strangers."

Ah…the first salvo. "And you would like me to buy them from you?"

Her eyes widened, the distaste in her expression blatant this time. "Don't be ridiculous. I simply need you to take a moment to identify which of the jewelry are heirlooms. If you don't have the time, perhaps your mother would be willing to do it. Anyway, I can't and I want to make sure your family takes possession of them before I dispose of the others."

"You propose to *give* me the family pieces?"

"Yes." She looked at him as if she was doubting his intelligence.

It was a new experience for him and he almost found himself smiling.

"It would actually help quite a bit if someone could go through all of the things in her bedroom with me to make sure anything of sentimental value to the family is kept before I have the removalists come."

"Removalists?"

"I've been in contact with an international association dedicated to the welfare of children. They've agreed to take possession of Andrea's things and sell them at auction to raise funds for their cause."

Reeling with the unexpected direction the conversation had taken, Sebastian's superior brain took several seconds to compute the import of Rachel's words. "You don't plan to keep *anything* of your mother's?"

"No." Rachel's now completely dispassionate expression told him nothing of her thoughts.

"But her clothes alone are easily worth over one-hundred-thousand American dollars."

"That's wonderful news for the charity."

"But means nothing to you?" He refused to believe it. No one was this uninterested in financial gain. "And the apartment in New York. You plan to give that to charity as well?"

"She owned an apartment in New York?"

Rachel sounded more annoyed than overjoyed by that piece of news.

"I suppose you're going to tell me you want to donate that to charity as well?" he asked derisively.

"No, of course not."

"I didn't think so."

"If you'll have the deed drawn up, I'll sign it back over to the estate."

Sebastian reared to his feet, sending his chair crashing backward. "What kind of game are you playing?"

Rachel paled, but drew herself up, uncrossing her legs and moving forward on her chair.

"I'm not playing any sort of game," she said with quiet vehemence. "Maybe you were right about me trying to put a brake on Andrea's behavior. I *didn't* try and I'll have to live with that knowledge for the rest of my life, but I refuse to personally profit by it. I simply won't." The fervor in Rachel's manner was either the best drama he'd seen in a long time, or she was entirely sincere.

"There is no need for you to make a grand gesture," he dismissed with irritation, realizing his words the day before had instigated this conversation. "While there is no doubt your mother manipulated my uncle for her own gain, her material extravagance cost him negligibly in a financial sense."

He listed off the few properties and cars Andrea had been gifted by Matthias in their six year long marriage.

None of which did Sebastian have any desire to take possession of. It had been the *personal cost* of marriage to the grasping woman that had hurt Matthias and subsequently his family so much.

"Then it should be a simple matter for your lawyers to see that all significant properties are returned to the estate and smaller possessions donated to charity."

"My uncle would not have wanted you to give up claim to your inheritance in some misguided attempt to make up for the past and I refuse to condone you doing so."

She shook her head and smiled, a genuinely amused expression that made her green eyes glow and his breathing go from normal to erratic.

"You are so used to getting your own way, you amaze me."

"Is that so?" He wasn't sure if her words were a condemnation or not.

"Yes. You're absolutely confident that you can dictate my decisions for me." Her lips still twitched with humor.

"And you find this amusing?"

Her lips tucked into a prim bow. "Not really, it's merely that it apparently has not occurred to you, but *it's up to me* how I dispose of Andrea's property. If you refuse to accept reversion to the estate, then I will donate it all to worthy causes." Without warning, the amusement drained from her expression. "I want nothing of my mother's. Nothing at all."

"It is too late. You carry her genes." The cynical words were out before he thought better of them and he cursed in Greek as Rachel's face leached of all color.

She stood up, a visible tremor in her limbs, her eyes burning him with indictment for the pain he saw there. "If you don't have the necessary papers for me to sign before I leave Greece, I will see to the disposal of the properties when I return to America."

She turned and walked from the room, ignoring his demand she wait. He watched her go, frustration gripping his insides.

Damn it all to hell. Why had he said that?

Rachel had come into his uncle's study and set all of Sebastian's preconceived ideas on their head. She had proven in the most basic way that her mother's influence over her values and actions was negligible and still he had taunted her with being Andrea's daughter.

It had been unfair and obviously painful to her.

He could not remember the last time he had apologized to a woman, but he was sure he needed to offer one now.

Rachel sat across from Phillippa Kouros and wondered why she'd talked herself into joining the family for dinner. She'd felt rude asking for yet another meal to be served in her room and then there had been the message from Sebastian.

He'd sent a servant to inform her he expected her to share the meal with the family.

And she'd come, not wanting to offend him.

Why did she care what the judgmental tyrant thought of her? He'd shown her that despite his kindness in the past, just like everyone else, he saw her through a glass tinted by her mother's bad blood. So what if he was the one man she'd ever felt a physical reaction to?

Her adolescent fantasies of him as the hero of her dreams were just that and she needed to vanquish those images forever from her brain.

Which meant she should be doing her best to complete the break with the Kouros and Demakis families.

Nevertheless, she found herself trying to draw his mother into conversation. The older woman's dark eyes were too sad for Rachel's tender heart to ignore.

Sebastian had been called from the table to take an urgent international call at the beginning of dinner. His brother had left the island with the rest of the family after the wills had been read.

"I've only got a small patio at my apartment, but I keep an herb garden," Rachel said as the salad course was served.

Phillippa's great passion was gardening and Rachel gave silent thanks for something to talk about unrelated to the family's recent loss.

"Basil and mint grow especially well in pots," Phillippa replied, her dulled eyes lighting a little with interest. "I had not expected you to like gardening. Andrea was appalled by the very idea of getting dirt on her hands."

"My mother and I shared very little in common."

"That is unfortunate."

"Yes." What else could she say?

"A mother and a daughter can find much joy in sharing one another's lives. My own mother taught me many things, not least of which was a love of growing things."

"She must have been a very special woman."

"She was. She and Uncle Matthias were always close." The grief came back to settle over Phillippa like a physical mantle.

"Did you teach your sons to garden?" Rachel

honestly couldn't imagine Sebastian or Aristide tending plants, but she hoped the question would get Phillippa's mind off of her grief.

The older woman smiled with indulgence. "No. Those two were always too busy for such a time intensive hobby." She shook her head. "I have two wonderful sons, but I would have liked having a daughter as well."

"I'm sure when they marry, their wives will find you a welcome addition to their lives."

The thought of Sebastian married to a proper Greek girl caused pain deep in the region of her heart, but Rachel disregarded it. She had grown very adept at ignoring her feelings.

But Phillippa was shaking her head again. "They were too busy as boys for hobbies and are too busy as men making money to find wives. Sebastian is already thirty and he has never even dated a woman longer than a few weeks."

"I'm sure when the time is right…" Her voice trailed off at the strange look in the older woman's dark eyes.

But before she could question it, Sebastian returned from his telephone call.

He folded his tall frame into the chair at the end of the table. "Mama, there is something I would appreciate you doing for Rachel."

The Greek woman looked at her son with obvious love and approval. "What is it, my son?"

"She wants to donate her mother's possessions to auction for charity, but she doesn't want anything of sentimental value to the family to be sold." He looked to Rachel as if expecting her to confirm or deny his words.

So, she nodded. "That's right."

Phillippa's dark brown eyes expressed her surprise. "You wish me to go through your mother's things with you?"

"Just the things in her room. Anything that might be considered hers in the other rooms of the house can simply stay with the villa." She'd thought about it and that seemed the easiest way to handle the situation.

"But surely you'll want the things she treasured."

"No."

"I have a few items of my mother's. They give me comfort when I think of her."

"I will find more satisfaction knowing her possessions brought something good to the lives of children in need."

The compassionate understanding in Phillippa's eyes was almost enough to make Rachel lose the rigid hold she had on her emotions. "I understand. I would be pleased to help you."

"Thank you," Rachel replied with deep sincerity.

The sweet fragrance of honeysuckle mingled with the warm, salt laden air off the sea, wrapping around Rachel while her toes sank into pebbly sand. Unable to sleep, she'd come down to the beach, thinking a walk would help settle her mind.

But it wasn't her mind that needed settling.

It was her body.

Being around Sebastian always did this to her, made her aware of her femininity in a way she managed to ignore the rest of the time. After what had happened to her when she was sixteen, that wasn't hard, but somehow the powerful tycoon undermined defenses that were rock-solid around other men.

And he didn't even try.

Sebastian Kouros had no interest in her, had never once intimated that he was aware of her as anything other than his beloved great-uncle's stepdaughter.

But that didn't stop her hormones from raging, or her heart from tying itself in knots over him.

"What are you doing out here, *pethi mou?*"

Spinning around at the sound of his voice, her heart climbed right up into her throat. She staggered backward away from that all too close masculine body, her feet hitting wet sand and then water. "Sebastian!"

His hands shot out and grabbed her shoulders, stopping her from an ignominious landing in the shallow water. "You did not know I was here?"

She shook her head dumbly.

He pulled her forward until her feet were once again on dry land, but he did not move, leaving her way too close to him. "I made no attempt to disguise my approach."

"I w-was thinking." She stumbled over her words, her brain processing the new sensory input from his arrival.

His fingers were warm and solid through the silk-thin cotton of her sleeves and his scent, spicy and overwhelmingly male, dominated her senses. The full moon supplied sufficient light for his formfitting, black T-shirt to reveal every defined abdomen and well-developed chest muscle. While his light colored sports shorts drew attention to legs that would have looked more appropriate on a long-distance runner than a corporate executive. His feet were bare like hers and their toes were scant inches apart.

For some reason that seemed very intimate.

CHAPTER TWO

"YOU must have been thinking about something very absorbing if your thoughts were so deep they prevented you from hearing my footsteps."

How ironic that thoughts of the man had prevented her from preparing herself mentally to meet up with him. "Yes."

"Why are you not sleeping?"

Did he realize he was still holding on to her? She tried shrugging to see if the movement would remind him to release her and step back. "I couldn't."

He ignored her silent bid for freedom, probably hadn't even noticed it. "Your mother died less than a week ago. It is understandable, this lack of rest."

"I suppose," she replied, content to let him draw his own conclusions.

She had enough to deal with not moving those remaining inches and snuggling into the warmth and safety his tall body offered. She wanted him physically and that in itself was shocking enough, but she wanted something else from him, something she'd learned long ago was not on offer in her life. Love. Commitment. Security.

"I understand. My uncle's death has caused much grief in my family."

That was probably as close as Sebastian would come to admitting his own weakness and the fact he was no doubt awake because of his own undiluted grief. Any feelings of sadness she had at the death of her mother were weakened by relief that the emotional pain of living in the shadow of her misdeeds was over.

She licked her lips, trying to maintain her concentration when his nearness was wreaking havoc with her ability to focus on what was being said. "Matthias was a good man."

Sebastian's hands dropped away from her shoulders finally, but he remained too close to ease her awkwardness. "He was, but I should not have dismissed your own grieving."

"What do you mean?" She had not expressed any real grief, so how could he have dismissed it?

She wasn't even sure if she was capable of mourning her mother's death.

"I was not kind to you this afternoon and I am sorry." The words came out stilted, not at all like his usual smooth conversation.

He probably apologized about as often as she dated, which was never.

"It's no big deal. Don't worry about it."

"I hurt you and I should not have added to your pain in that way."

Oh, man, when he got going on the remorse thing, he took it seriously. And it made her feel guilty because while he'd hurt her, it had not been in addition to the pain of loss, but to the pain of a lifetime lived as Andrea's daughter.

"Thank you for your concern, but honestly, I'm used to comments like that."

The sound he made said her words had not soothed him.

She sighed, unable to stifle the urge to reach out, to touch in an age-old gesture of comfort. Her fingers settled gently against his hair roughened arm and it was all she could do to remember what she was going to say. Oh, yeah…

"I'm not angry with you." Not anymore. "Matthias was a kind and caring man. I'm sorry he died the way he did. I'm sorry my mother's life ended the way it did, but I don't blame you for pointing out the truth. I am her daughter and I've learned to live with that."

An indecipherable expression settled over his angular features. "Earlier, I was worried you might take your story to the tabloids, but I realize now you would not do so."

Chills of horror skated along her nerve endings. *"Never."*

"Andrea courted publicity of the worst kind."

"And I had to live with it all my life."

"You did not like it."

"I hated it. As a child, I got teased and was expelled from two different private schools because of her behavior." Andrea had been caught having sex with one of Rachel's teachers by the man's wife and the second time, she'd been arrested for cocaine possession. "It wasn't much better at university. The world seems like such a big place until you're the one in the middle of ugly media attention."

And by then, her mother had married a rich Greek tycoon old enough to be her father. It was the stuff of fantasy for would-be journalists making their name in the tabloid press.

Which was why Rachel had legally changed her last name upon graduation. She'd never told Andrea, not wanting a big scene, but no one in Rachel's current life knew that she was related to a woman notorious for her sexual exploits and questionable social activities.

In the United States, the story of Rachel Long, daughter of Andrea Long Demakis, simply did not exist.

Being shy and rather average looking had its advantages.

She realized this time it was she who continued to hold on to him and quickly pulled her hand away. "Sorry."

"I do not mind."

She swallowed. "Yes, well, I should get back. I'm sure I can sleep now," she said, lying through her teeth, but needing to get away from his unnerving presence.

His hands caught her waist, halting her body and her breathing all in one go. "Are you sure?"

"I…" She choked trying to get air into her lungs and he pulled her closer, soothing her back, his expression too heated to be labeled concern.

She started to breathe again, but still couldn't speak. His silver gaze was doing things to her insides she'd long since convinced herself was the stuff of fantasy. Shivery sensations traveled along nerve endings she didn't even know she had and a heavy, aching sensation in her womb radiated downward to make her thighs clench.

Firm, masculine lips tilted in a knowing smile and she was sure he knew just what was happening to her.

He never broke eye contact as he drew her near until their bodies barely touched and she could not help the involuntary shudder that went through her at contact.

His eyes filled with primal male triumph. "Yes. I knew you felt it too."

"Felt what?" she asked, knowing her attempt at prevarication was hopeless.

He ignored it completely.

"I need to know." His head lowered until his lips were a breath from hers. "Don't you wonder too?"

She would have asked, "Wonder what?", but his mouth closed over hers.

And she stopped thinking.

All she could do was feel.

It was entirely alien, this merging of their mouths, the mingling of their breath, the gentle seduction of knowing lips. She had not known men like him, with so much power and masculine strength, could be gentle.

Her hands went to his chest of their own accord, drawn by a lure as inexplicable as it was inescapable. She tentatively explored the ridges of muscle that had fascinated her earlier and her fingertips encountered hard points. Mesmerized by this unexpected indicator of his excitement, she investigated the phenomena completely.

He groaned and yanked her into his body, his hold growing fierce, the kiss turning incendiary. Fiery passion sizzled between their lips and she did not pull away. That fact registered with what was left of her conscious mind along with the realization she felt not one iota of fear.

There was no room inside her for anything but an all-consuming erotic craving and physical delight, both sparked by him. He tasted good, so different from her and yet infinitely right and desirable.

Without really knowing how it had happened, his tongue was in her mouth and he was teaching her how to find pleasure in an intimate kiss she had always considered much too invasive. She wanted to give it back and copied his movements with instinctive feminine sensuality she had been sure she no longer possessed.

Growling, he lifted her off the sand, grinding his pelvis against hers and causing shock waves to ripple throughout her body.

But still, she felt no trepidation…nothing that would dilute the molten lava of need flowing through her veins.

When he pressed against her bottom, causing her thighs to drift apart, it was the most natural thing in the world to lift her legs and lock her ankles tight behind his back. Her skirt rucked up, leaving her skin bare against him in an unbearably exciting connection and sexual hunger exploded inside her as her sweet spot rubbed against his hardened male flesh.

She needed *something* and she pressed herself against him as intimately as possible, gyrating her hips to increase the sensations exploding in her most intimate flesh.

His hand trespassed the silk of her panties to touch a place that had not been touched in seven years. The feel of his fingertip at the entrance to her body brought forth a rush of dew drenched pleasure. Then his finger moved to possess her and old fear rushed through her in an unstoppable torrent, dousing her pleasure and filling her with a desperate need to be free.

She tore her mouth from his. "No. Stop. *What are we doing?*"

"You do not know?" he asked incredulously, his voice thick with desire.

She didn't answer. Could not answer. The feel of that finger almost inside her had brought forth memories that would drown her if she let them.

Unlocking her ankles, she frantically tried to scramble from his arms.

After a second of unequal struggling, he let her go, spewing words in Greek she had no desire to know the translation for.

"I'm sorry," she jerked out, yanking her skirt down to cover her wobbly legs.

Her heart was beating her to death, her palms were damp and her mouth was cottony and dry.

His hands clenched and she stepped back, unable to prevent a reaction born of the past but called forth in the present.

His face a mask of frustrated desire, he threw

his head back and inhaled deeply before looking at her again.

When he did, the feral intensity had been muted, but his mouth was set in a grim line. "No. It is I who should apologize. A man should not take advantage of a woman's weak emotional state. It was wrong to kiss you when you were already upset from the week's events."

She couldn't believe he was taking it on himself, but then hadn't she always known he was no common man? He stood above all others in her mind and had been elevated to almost saint status with his understanding of her rejection.

He didn't know why she had pulled back and had not asked, creating a well of gratitude that ran soul deep inside her.

"I didn't mean to let it go that far," she said, remembering accusations from the past of being a tease, tormenting words that haunted her nightmares.

"I did not mean for it to happen *at all*," he admitted ruefully, making her smile when it should have been impossible. "I saw you from my room and came out to check on you and to apologize for my inappropriate remark earlier. Instead, I took advantage of an attraction neither of us would benefit from acting on."

While his words completely exonerated her from blame and set her mind at ease, they left gaping wounds in her heart. He was saying that they did not belong together in any sense.

She'd known that.

Had always understood he was way out of her league, but it still hurt. He'd given her her first taste of real passion and the possibility she could know the entire gamut of sexual experience with him tantalized her. She'd gotten frightened, but only when he touched her like she'd been touched that one fateful night.

If she could tell him about it…ask him to avoid doing that, would she be able to make love completely without fear?

Why was she even asking herself these questions? He had made no secret of the fact that he was appalled by the fact he'd kissed her. Sexual intimacy with Sebastian Kouros was not on the cards for her.

She forced her lips into a semblance of a smile. "You're right. A relationship between the two of us would be out of the question." She was trying to sound sophisticated and casually accepting of his reading of the situation, but she was afraid the façade would crack any second. "I—I think, I'll go to bed now."

He insisted on walking her to her room, not relieving her of his now grim presence until she shut the door on his formal goodnight.

Sebastian walked away from Rachel's room calling himself six kinds of a fool. What in the hell had he been thinking to kiss her like that?

To kiss her at all?

Okay, so he had wanted her for years, but she was not the woman for him. Not even for a brief affair. She might be different from Andrea, but Rachel was still daughter to a piranha.

As well, it would hurt his family if he got involved with her. They deserved better than a second serving of the kind of gossip that had surrounded Matthias's marriage. He had loved his great-uncle very much, but the old man had been ruled by his libido when it came to Andrea and he had brought shame upon their family.

How could a Greek man with any kind of pride stay married to a woman he knew to be unfaithful?

And yet Matthias had.

The night of the crash had not been the first time his uncle had found evidence of his much younger wife's sexual exploits outside the bounds of their marriage. Each time, Sebastian had been sure the old man would finally come to his senses and kick the bitch out of his life, but Matthias never had.

Sebastian would never allow a woman to make such a fool of him. He had no tolerance for lies and subterfuge of the type that had marked Matthias's second marriage. He abhorred any type of dishonesty and would not give the time of day to a woman who lied about her age, much less her fidelity.

His great-uncle had been smart enough to

prevent his beautiful, conscience-less wife from cleaning him out financially and had shown his brain was still functioning on some level within the bounds of his marriage in not leaving her anything in his will, but there was no doubt Andrea Demakis had bankrupted the old man's pride.

For a Greek male, that was the worst consequence imaginable.

Sebastian had found it impossible to comprehend Matthias's willingness to stay married. How could he have allowed himself to be manipulated by his sexuality into pursuing a lifestyle the total antithesis of what he had known his first sixty-plus years? A man should live his final years with dignity, but his uncle had not.

Humiliation had been his companion, particularly for the past year. What had spurred Andrea to wave her sexual conquests in her elderly husband's face? What had made her behave so foully? And why had Rachel ignored it all, never once attempting to stop the abhorrent behavior?

The dark night outside his bedroom window

offered no answers, but the questions served to remind him that no matter how different Rachel appeared on the surface, she had been too self-interested to care about Matthias Demakis.

Just like her mother.

Rachel finished packing the last box in her mother's bedroom and closed it. A sense of accomplishment warred with disappointment. She'd searched Andrea's room thoroughly and found nothing related to her life before she married Matthias Demakis. No indication of who the man who had fathered Rachel might be.

Considering her mother's taste in companions, she would have given up her desire to find him years ago but for two poignant memories from her childhood.

She'd been little, three, maybe four, and sitting on a man's lap. He'd been reading to her and while she had no idea what he'd been reading, she could still remember the sense of love and security she'd felt. She'd called him, "Daddy," and kissed his cheek when he'd finished. He'd hugged her tight and when she closed her eyes she could remember that hug.

It had made her feel safe.

And she remembered waking in the night and searching an apartment in the dark for her daddy, crying and calling his name. She'd been about five, or six then. Her mother had slept on, no doubt passed out from alcohol or something more potent, but Rachel had stayed up all night, accepting that her daddy wasn't coming back only when the first rays of sun indicated a new day.

She didn't know if her father had chosen to stay out of their lives as her mother had claimed or if he had been unable to find them. Andrea and Rachel had lived in various parts of Europe since Rachel had started school. Her mother's exploits had made the gutter press at times, but wouldn't have been noteworthy in the States. She had been neither filthy rich, until Matthias, nor a celebrity.

Even her marriage to Matthias Demakis had only made her of interest to a few gossip rags in the States. While other students at her university had learned enough about her exploits to judge Rachel on them, that didn't mean a man who hadn't seen Andrea in over twenty years would recognize her in publicized photos, or even read that type of paper.

Rachel wanted to believe her father was an American man, unaware of Andrea's recent notoriety and longtime residence in Europe. However, she had to acknowledge that he could very well be as permanently gone as Andrea.

Shaking off thoughts that led nowhere, Rachel ran tape along the box's seam. For *whatever reason,* her father was lost to her and that was that. She tore the tape off and straightened, blowing at a strand of hair that had fallen from her ponytail. Emotionally detached, she surveyed the once decadent room now stripped of much of its sumptuous decor.

Sebastian had encouraged her to pack everything for the auction. He planned to redo the room in the near future, erasing Andrea's influence on the villa as thoroughly as possible. Of course, that's not how he'd put it. He'd been very tactful since their discussion in the study three days ago, but his feelings regarding Andrea Demakis were no secret.

Stretching tired muscles, Rachel reached toward the ceiling and then bent from one side to the other. Her muscles ached and her eyes burned with fatigue. She'd spent a lot of time on her knees packing and sorting in the past three days and had slept poorly at night, too much time given to reliving Sebastian's kiss.

Bending forward, she touched her fingertips to the plush carpeting. Straightening, she leaned backward, doing almost a backbend, and saw a pair of trouser covered male legs.

The Greek curse that met her ears was instantly recognizable and just as startling.

Her balance gave way and she could do nothing to stop falling flat on her back, bumping her head in the process.

Sebastian dropped to his knee beside her, his gorgeous features set in concerned lines. "Are you all right, *pedhaki mou?*"

She couldn't speak, her breath having been

knocked right out of her. The best she could do was a series of guppy-like movements with her lips.

Strong hands gripped her shoulders and gently pulled her into a sitting position, causing a whoosh of air to make its way into her lungs.

"Thank you," she croaked out.

He probed the back of her head with his fingertips. "Does this hurt?"

"Just a little."

"There is no bump forming."

"I'm all right."

He didn't release her, but continued checking for injuries in a way that left her trembly with want. "What were you doing?"

She felt heat blister her cheeks while she tried to control the urge to touch back. "Stretching."

"You fell."

"You surprised me," she informed him in a cranky tone that made her cringe inside. "I lost my balance."

"Ah, so it is my fault."

She tilted her head back to see his face, unable to credit the humor in his voice, but it was reflected in his molten metal eyes. So was a warmth she would do well to pretend was not there.

"Yes."

"Then I must do something to show my remorse at causing such a mishap."

Her jaw locked against any word she might have uttered as his mouth came down to meet her own.

It was not a flaming kiss, had no overt passion in it, but nevertheless, her heart went wild and her body ached to align itself with his.

Thankfully, his hold on her shoulders was too strong to allow her to do it and humiliate herself in the process.

He lifted his head. "You have sweet lips, Rachel."

She licked them, tasting only him. "Thank you."

"So polite." He kissed her again, this time letting his lips linger for a few seconds, letting his tongue slip out to gently mesh with her own.

He pulled back far enough to speak. "Have I made up for my transgression?"

His breath brushed her lips tantalizingly and she wanted to continue the kiss, but she forced out a choked, "Yes."

"That is unfortunate."

Oh, man…this guy was one-hundred percent lethal. "Y-yes, it is."

"Maybe I should put something on account."

She couldn't say anything as his mouth came over hers again, but just as the kiss was turning wickedly interesting, Phillippa's voice came from the doorway.

"Is she all right, Sebastian? What happened?"

Making a low sound of frustration, he lifted his head and looked over his shoulder. "I startled her when she was stretching and she fell."

"I'm fine," Rachel added, prickling with hot embarrassment at having her clumsiness revealed as well as being caught kissing him.

"Are you sure? You are still on the floor."

Sebastian's laughter made his chest vibrate against Rachel and she felt herself falling further under his spell. "She is still on the floor because I have not let her up yet."

"Oh."

There was a wealth of meaning in that little word and it seemed to disturb Sebastian because his joviality disappeared and he made quick work of getting them both back on their feet and then stepping away from her. It felt like a rejection and she wanted to remind him he'd been the one to kiss her.

However, his white shirt showed smudges and wrinkles from her dusty hands where she'd unwittingly clutched at him and she had to admit, if only to herself, that she'd been a more than willing participant.

"Aristide is here. We will have lunch and then he will take me back to the mainland."

"You're leaving?" Rachel asked.

"Yes. I must get back to my garden."

"Thank you for your help with Andrea's things."

"It was my pleasure. You are a gentle young woman. I have been grieving my uncle's death and you kept my mind set on the present, not the past. It is I who owe you my thanks."

Rachel did not know how to react to the praise or the look of frowning interest Sebastian was bestowing on her. She felt like a moth in a jar and was finding it just as difficult to breathe.

"I like you," she finally managed to get out and Phillippa smiled.

"The feeling is mutual."

Thankfully, Sebastian said something about Rachel getting cleaned up before lunch and made it possible for her to make her escape.

Sebastian watched Rachel hurry from the room, her cheeks as red as ripe pomegranate seeds. "She does not know how to take a compliment."

"I imagine with her mother, she did not receive many," his mother replied as they made their way downstairs.

"No, I do not suppose she did."

"Andrea Demakis brought a great deal of pain to our family."

"Yes," he growled, wishing his body wasn't still reacting to holding Rachel in his arms.

His mother gave him one of those looks he'd never learned to decipher as they entered the dining room. "To be such a woman's daughter would have been even more painful."

"She did nothing to stem her mother's downward spiral this last year."

"Perhaps she felt she had no influence."

"Or she found her own comfort more important to her than that of an old man."

He had no trouble interpreting his mother's expression now. Disappointment radiated from her dark eyes and he gritted his teeth against justifying his accusation against Rachel. He had a feeling nothing he said would improve the situation.

He turned to greet his brother, but his mother was not finished with the conversation.

She walked around him to stand between him and his brother. "And does your personal comfort require you to drag her down to her mother's level in your mind so that you will not give in to the attraction you have for her?"

"I am not—"

His mother raised her hand. "Lie to yourself, my son, but do not attempt to lie to the woman who gave you birth. Rachel is not anything like Andrea, but if you believed that, your heart would be at risk and that frightens you."

That was going too far. *"I could never love the daughter of Andrea Demakis."*

"Uh-oh." His brother's expression was pained and his mother made a moue of distress.

Needing no further impetus, Sebastian turned toward the doorway.

Rachel stood, framed in its entry, wounded green eyes fixed on him.

CHAPTER THREE

SHE'D made an amazing transition in so short a time. Her straight brown hair was in a loose pile on top of her head and she'd changed into a dress that not only matched her eyes, but fit her more closely than her other clothing. The sage green silk highlighted the curves he'd been desperate to touch only minutes before and she'd glossed her bow-shaped lips. She looked beautiful and infinitely kissable.

Her expression said that would not be on offer again in this lifetime.

"I did not mean..." He drifted into silence for the first time in memory, not knowing what to say to undo the damage his hasty words had done.

She turned her head, breaking eye contact, her

body language dismissing him as effectively as if she had told him to go to hell.

"Would it be possible for you and Aristide to delay your departure an hour?" she asked his mother. "I could pack and go with you. I've finished sorting Andrea's things."

His mother shocked him by shaking her head with evident regret. "I am sorry, Rachel, but Aristide has an appointment he must keep. We will leave directly after lunch."

Aristide looked surprised as well, but he nodded. "That is right. I am sorry, Rachel."

"I could pack while the rest of you eat," Rachel offered.

Both the offer and her initial request infuriated Sebastian and he did not know why. "Surely that is not necessary. I will arrange for your transport to the mainland tomorrow morning."

"I would prefer to leave today." She didn't bother to look at him as she said it.

"You have no reason to fear staying alone in the villa with me."

She turned then and her gaze flayed him. "You've made that clear enough."

"Come, let us eat lunch. Rachel, you do not wish to pack in a rush. That invariably leads to leaving something behind."

Rachel sighed, looking unhappy, but accepting. "You are right. I won't be returning to the island, so I will have to make sure I take everything with me this time."

"You will always be welcome here." His mother's tone brooked no argument. "After all, this was your home for several years."

"It is Sebastian's home now and I wouldn't dream of intruding on him in the future."

Aristide came around the table, stepping in front of Sebastian to lead Rachel to a seat.

"Visits from family are never an intrusion," he said with a charming smile Sebastian had an inexplicable urge to wipe off his brother's handsome, young face.

"You are kind to say so, but I am not family, not really, and I won't be coming back to Greece so the issue won't arise," she replied as she allowed him to seat her and then asked a question about his business, effectively changing the subject.

Sebastian had known in a vague way that once Rachel left, she would be gone for good, which was as it should be. He did not need the temptation of Andrea Demakis's daughter around, but hearing her say it with such certainty inexplicably angered him.

Rachel did her best to ignore Sebastian during lunch, focusing her attention on his younger brother and Phillippa. Aristide was very charming, flirting shamelessly with her and keeping them all entertained with an account of one of his friend's visit to Crete.

Sebastian smoldered, but she could not imagine why. What did he care if she enjoyed a harmless flirtation with Aristide?

Sebastian had been so adamant she was not worthy of his affection and she'd felt so *stupid* for allowing herself to give in to the urge to dress up a little for lunch, to try to look pretty for *him*.

A man who could kiss her senseless one minute and the next declare with positive vehemence that he would never feel any sort of emotion for her. What a laugh.

She was such an idiot.

She wished she could have left with the younger man and Phillippa, but that was not possible. Sebastian's mother was right. Rachel would no doubt regret attempting to pack in haste. Not that she would contact Sebastian to send anything on for her, no matter what might get left behind.

However, she supposed she could avoid Sebastian until the following morning when the launch came for her.

Rachel was on the beach attempting to do just that a few hours later.

She dug her toes into the sand, enjoying the warmth of the late afternoon sun. It was the first time in three days she'd really relaxed. She'd spent the time since lunch packing her own things, making sure she'd cleaned out every nook and cranny of the room that had been hers since she was seventeen.

And she was still berating herself. Because when she'd come across a small decorative box of mementos, she'd been unable to toss them and they were now packed in the corner of her biggest suitcase.

Inside the box were pictures she'd accumulated over the years since her mother's marriage to Matthias. Many of them were of Sebastian. Some were clippings from newspapers; some were photos from family gatherings she'd attended before finishing university. There was a single dried yellow rose from the bouquet he'd given her for her eighteenth birthday and the silver locket engraved with her initials he'd given her for her twenty-first.

There was even a black onyx cuff link he'd tossed in the study's trash bin when he'd lost the other one. She'd dug it out and put it away with her mementos. Such a silly, juvenile thing to do, but perhaps understandable as a teenager.

So, why had she felt the need to keep the cuff link at the age of twenty-three?

She didn't know. All she did know was that she had been unable to toss it and when she'd tried, she'd actually ended up pulling it out of the trash can in her bedroom to gently polish and put it back in the box. He'd worn the set of cuff links to her eighteenth birthday, the one and only time he'd ever danced with her.

She refused to analyze too closely why that had such emotional significance for her, just as she would not dwell on his forceful and public rejection earlier. Both issues were best left in the far recesses of her mind.

She yawned and lay back in the sand, letting tired muscles unwind. The quiet surrounded her, emphasizing the difference between the Southern Californian beaches back home and this one. No crashing surf or cacophony of voices rose to disturb her solitude. There were no horses for rent, or surfboards standing erect in the sand. The island was private and though a small village existed on the North side, the other occupants never trespassed on the Demakis Villa's beach.

She'd swum here unafraid of being ogled by men…when her mother was not entertaining.

Soon she would be leaving all this behind for good. She would not return to Greece, never see Sebastian again, never soak the sun's rays into her skin in quiet solitude like this one. Her heart contracted in rebellion of her thoughts.

"Eugenie informs me you plan to eat a snack in your room rather than join me for dinner."

Her eyes flew open to the sight of Sebastian towering over her reclining form. His hair covered, tanned legs dominated her line of sight and she had to tilt her head back to see his face. Like the other night, he'd changed into shorts, but his white polo shirt that emphasized the darkness of his skin went better with his power persona than the casual tank top had.

"What are you doing out here?"

"Obviously, I came to find you."

"Oh. Why?"

He frowned. "Is it really such a sacrifice to share your final meal in Greece with me?"

"I cannot imagine you wanting my company."

"Do not be foolish. You are a guest in my home."

And Greek hospitality was offended by the notion she would eat a solitary meal in her room. It had nothing to do with her, or him wanting to spend time with her. "Don't worry about me," she said, wanting to allay a guilt prompted evening *à deux*. "Entertainment is not required for my last night here."

His dark eyes traveled up and down her form, an expression in the gray depths she did not want to decipher and then he smiled. "Perhaps I wish to entertain you."

He was back to being the charming Greek billionaire, but she was still smarting from his vow he could never love Andrea Demakis's daughter and wanted none of it.

She clambered to her feet, brushing the sand off the seat of her loose fitting capris. "There's no need. I'm tired and could use the extra sleep of an early night."

"You cannot be thinking of going to bed now." He looked genuinely horrified as only a man who slept a mere five hours a night could. "It is barely evening."

"I'm hardly going to sleep right this minute." Though she was tired enough that the thought held some appeal. "But neither am I going to stay up for a typically late European dinner."

"Your flight is an early one?"

Why was he pushing this? Whether or not she spent her final night in his company could not really matter to him.

"I don't know," she admitted. "I wasn't sure how long it would take to sort through Andrea's things, so I didn't book my return flight in advance. I'll make reservations once I reach Athens tomorrow."

"What is the rush to leave then?"

She'd never been a game player and wasn't about to start now. "Sebastian, you don't want me here and I don't want to be here. That's reason enough, but there is also the fact I have to get back to work."

"I did not say I did not want you here."

No, he had merely said he could never love her. "I'm Andrea's daughter and you hated my mother."

"I hated the affect she had on my great-uncle, the way she stripped him of his dignity."

"Which can only mean the sooner I'm out of your hair the better you'll like it. You can forget Andrea and her daughter ever came into your family."

"I can never forget. It is because Andrea came into his life that Matthias is dead now."

"Then you definitely don't need a living reminder of your pain." She turned and started walking across the still warm sand, toward the steps leading up to the villa.

"Wait."

She ignored him. They'd said all that needed to be said.

Hard fingers wrapped around her wrist, halting her progress across the beach. "Damn it, I said *wait*."

She spun to face him, her emotions on the verge of exploding. "And I made it clear I don't want to. Now let me go."

She yanked at her wrist to no avail.

"I am sorry."

"I don't need an apology for the truth, *I just need you to leave me alone.*"

"My mother was pushing me into a corner and I didn't like it." His tone was driven, his cool shattered before her. "I'm not proud of saying something hurtful."

"What are you talking about?"

An impatient sound exploded from him. "You know very well. What you overheard me say at lunch."

She'd been reacting to his vow he couldn't forget her mother was the cause of his great-uncle's death. It had superceded the words she'd been working so hard all afternoon to sublimate, but they had to be faced now.

"Let me repeat, don't apologize for speaking the truth. It may hurt, but it's a clean wound and will heal faster than pain born of dishonesty." After a lifetime as Andrea's daughter Rachel knew the difference all too well.

His hand cupped her cheek, the touch oddly

protective. "And did it hurt to hear I could never love you?"

"Yes." She'd promised herself a long time ago to be as honest as it was possible for her to be. "Do we really need a postmortem?"

"I wish to know."

"Why, so you can gloat? Do you need to hear that I'm stupid enough to care about you so your ego is bolstered? Or maybe you just want some revenge for what you perceive as my dereliction of duty toward Matthias."

"It is not that."

"I don't understand you, Sebastian." She swallowed against the constriction in her throat. "*You* kissed *me* in Andrea's room. And the other night, you kissed me on the beach and *touched me*. We almost made love, for goodness' sake, but then you told your mother you could *never* love *me*."

His hand traveled down her cheek and neck, one finger softly brushing the rapid pulse he found there. "Sex is not love."

She flinched from the physical pain of those

words. "No, it's not," she said barely above a whisper.

She might have almost no personal experience in that area, but she'd seen enough growing up to know he spoke an irrefutable truth. Another bit of honesty that hurt because his words confirmed that any feelings he had for her were limited to the physical.

"I want you."

"I'm not my mother." Sex was not a disposable commodity for Rachel and she hated it that he would relegate something so devastating to her to nothing more than the slaking of a base desire.

"No, you are not."

She pulled away, not believing him for a second. He'd said too much to the contrary in the last four days. "I need to go."

"I want you to spend the night with me."

Her mouth opened, but nothing came out. Every word he spoke was like a knife slashing her heart and her hope was bleeding to death. *"No."*

"I did not mean it." His face was creased with lines of frustration.

"You *don't* want to spend the night with me?" she asked with blatant sarcasm that hurt her as much as it mocked him.

"I assure you that I do, but *I did not mean what I told my mother."*

"Is sex really worth compromising your personal integrity?" Or maybe he didn't consider it wrong to lie to Andrea Demakis's daughter.

"It is not like that."

"Of course it is."

"Please, Rachel."

Her mouth froze in open astonishment the he would plead. "What is it like then?" she heard herself asking.

"My feelings for you cannot be dismissed simply because you are the daughter of a woman who brought my family grief."

"Of course they can. It's the Greek way." A concept of vengeance as old as the story of Nemesis.

"No, they cannot." It was as if the admission

was dragged out of him and that more than anything else made her believe it.

"You have feelings for me?" she choked out.

His jaw tightened. "Have dinner with me; spend the evening as my companion."

Admissions of emotion were over it seemed, but he had said the words. His feelings could not be dismissed.

"And tomorrow?"

"You have no plane reservations."

"But…"

"You do not have to leave right away."

"I—"

He pressed his finger to her lips. "Shh…do not think." His eyes were hotter than the scorching sun. "The past is gone, but we exist here in the present and I want to explore what it is between us."

She could no more deny him than she'd been able to throw away her memories surrounding him. "All right."

His smile stole her breath and then his lips finished the job, closing over hers with a drugging sensuality that left her dazed long after he walked her to her room and left her there to get ready for their dinner *date.*

She wore a dress Andrea had bought her, one she had left behind in Greece when she went to America. It was short, falling to three inches above her knee in a sophisticated black crepe, leaving her arms bare and though the neckline was demure, it clung revealingly to her breasts.

She would be horribly uncomfortable wearing it with another man, but Sebastian was different, even after everything that had transpired since the funeral. She was coming to accept that he always would be. To her.

Which was why she was willing to explore this thing between them. If it wasn't Sebastian, she was sure it would never be anyone else. Not only because of what had happened to her when she was sixteen, but because the emotional connection she had to him had grown over years she had tried to starve it, staying away from Greece and the island.

What were the chances they would diminish

altogether, even if she never saw him again? Nil. And if she cared for him, she wasn't going to fall for someone else.

She didn't want to.

Besides, he'd said he had feelings for her and for a guy like Sebastian, so proud and self-contained, that was a huge admission.

She took extra care with her makeup and hair, brushing it until it was like dark liquid silk and then pulling it into a classic French twist that added to the sophistication of her outfit.

As she stood outside the drawing room, she couldn't help remembering what a fool she'd felt earlier dressing up for him and then hearing him say he could never love her. Maybe dressing this way had been a mistake. She should go change. Right now, before he saw her.

He looked at her as she tensed, ready to leave, and there was no mistaking the blatant male appreciation in his eyes. Her fears melted under the heat of his appraisal. He motioned to her to come to him and she started walking as if led by an invisible string.

When she reached him, he leaned down and kissed both her cheeks, his hands warm on her bare shoulders. "You look beautiful."

"Thank you."

He looked pretty darn gorgeous himself in a dark suit, tailored to fit his muscular structure to a T. He wore a tie, something he rarely did to dinner at home with the family and she realized he'd dressed up for her as well.

She smiled.

He got her a drink and then Eugenie called them into dinner. They spent the meal talking, their discussion surprisingly easy and diverse.

"So, why do you work as an accountant?"

"Why not be an accountant?" she quipped, sipping from her wineglass, feeling more relaxed with him than she ever had.

"You used to paint."

"I still do."

"So, why not work in a job that calls on your creativity?"

"I like my job. It's not too demanding and the environment is peaceful."

"Would not an artist's studio be just as peaceful?"

"I'm not that good. Besides, it's almost impossible to make a living as an artist." And she'd realized early on that she needed a steady source of income if she was going to make a life different and separate from her mother's.

"Matthias would have supported you."

She physically shuddered at the thought. The cost would have been much too high. Living with Andrea. "I didn't want to be supported. I wanted to make my own way."

"That is commendable." There was something in his tone she didn't quite get.

"Thank you. I really do like my job though. Numbers are reliable and they don't throw temper tantrums."

"Do you?"

"There's only room for one drama queen in a family. Andrea was ours. I'm pretty even tempered."

He looked at her, as if assessing things about her she did not even know about herself. "I wonder."

"Have you ever seen me have a fit?" she demanded, a little irritated he would question her assessment of herself.

Their argument earlier did not count. It had been mutual, not a diva temper tantrum and she had been blatantly provoked.

"No, but I had never seen you react with passion before the other night on the beach either."

"It's not the same."

He shrugged as if the subject did not matter to him. "Perhaps not."

But a little later, the conversation came back to her job.

"You cannot meet many men working for a woman's fitness center?" he asked.

"No." And she liked it that way.

"I am glad."

"Why is that?'"

"I am a possessive man."

"But I don't belong to you."

"Don't you?"

Honesty in this instance, even with herself, would cost too much. The thought of belonging to a man who would never belong to her was hardly confidence building, so she ignored the question. "How long are you staying on the island?"

"For a few more days only. I must get back to Athens."

"Your company is suffering?"

"I employ proficient management and I am not unconnected here. I continue to work remotely, but to do so indefinitely would be bad business."

"Why *are* you staying?" She doubted he was seeing to the disposal of his great-uncles clothing personally.

"You cannot guess?"

"It's that whole Greek hospitality thing I guess." After all, his mother had been staying until that morning and then there was Rachel.

"I had more reason than a need to play good host."

"You didn't want Andrea's daughter to make off with the silver in your absence?"

He didn't laugh as she expected him to, but shook his head, his expression pretty grim.

"Then why?"

"You are here. I find I cannot help wanting to be here as well." He didn't look very happy about the fact, but even so, his words touched her deeply.

"It's a compulsion." And she was glad she wasn't the only one affected by it.

He frowned, but his eyes made her insides shiver. "Yes. It is."

After dinner, he led her out onto the terrace where the soft, bluesy music from the stereo filled the sultry air.

He tugged her into his arms. "Dance with me."

She hadn't danced with him, or anyone else since her eighteenth birthday, but he wasn't asking her to waltz a complicated step around the terrace. His hands were linked loosely just above her tailbone and he was swaying slowly to the sensual beat.

Letting her hands slide up inside his suit jacket to rest against his chest, she relaxed into full body contact. Her conscious mind which told her such a move was unwise could not maintain sway against instincts clamoring for supremacy. It felt so good to be held by him and unreal. It was the sense of unreality that made it all seem so safe.

Logic said that Sebastian Kouros could have any woman he wanted. He was gorgeous. He was sexy. And he was probably five times as wealthy as his great-uncle had been. The perfect catch, he would never let himself get overly involved with Rachel, no matter how strong the compulsion he felt to be with her. He was too cautious.

And she was Andrea Demakis's daughter.

One song segued into another, their bodies in complete accord and her nerve endings sizzled with slow burning pleasure. He was affected as well. The evidence pressed against her stomach while his hands sank lower and lower until they were cupping her bottom with gentle intensity.

Their dancing, if you could call it that, reduced to nothing more than a slow movement from side to side as feminine and masculine flesh brushed profoundly against each other. Her cheek rested against his chest and she could hear the steady, strong beat of his heart. She rubbed her face up and down, enjoying the smooth, rich fabric of his shirt, loving the springy hair behind it.

She was in a state of dazed enchantment when he unexpectedly set her away from him, his expression rueful. "If I do not send you to bed, I will end up joining you."

She swayed, wanting him to do just that.

"When you come to my bed, you will be sure you want to be there."

He'd said when, not if, but she wasn't going to chastise his arrogance. *She was ready to go now.* Even knowing it was probably emotional suicide, only the fear that she would balk at the final gate kept her from saying so.

Sebastian stood below the ice-cold shower and cursed his own stupidity. He didn't know which was dumber, letting himself get so worked up sexually, or not taking advantage of Rachel's obvious willingness.

Why the hell had he insisted on her staying in the first place?

Compulsion.

She'd said it, but the word was his. His desire for Rachel Long was a compulsion he could not ignore. He wanted her and he was going to have her, but it was more than physical need driving him and that bothered him.

Sex he could handle.

Emotion, the kind found between a man and a woman, had no place in his life.

CHAPTER FOUR

THE next three days were sheer paradise for Rachel.

She and Sebastian spent the mornings together, swimming and exploring the island. He even took her fishing and laughed when she refused to bait the hook, but still managed to catch more fish than he did. The afternoons and early evenings were reserved for work. Then they ate dinner together and spent most every evening in one another's company until finding their separate beds.

They kept strictly away from discussing her mother and his great-uncle, which meant they stayed off the past altogether. It also meant she didn't tell him about what happened when she was sixteen.

She wondered if she should, but the more time they spent together, the more convinced she became that she would have no problem engaging in sexual intimacy with him. She didn't really want to talk about that dark time, so she made no effort to break the unspoken moratorium Sebastian had placed on discussing the past.

Phillippa called the first day and upon learning that Rachel was still on the island, insisted on speaking to her. After that, they spoke each afternoon. Rachel really enjoyed her chats with Sebastian's mother. Phillippa treated Rachel like a valued friend, almost like a member of the family and she liked that.

At some point, she would have to return to work, but she couldn't make herself contemplate leaving Sebastian and the relationship growing between them.

On the fourth morning after Phillippa left, Sebastian came to the breakfast table, his jaw taut and his eyes reflecting tension.

"What's the matter?" she asked after he leaned over to kiss her square on the mouth.

He did that a lot. Kissing her, but he never pushed for more and while part of her appreciated his restraint, she couldn't help wondering the why of it.

"I have business in Athens and must fly out today."

Her heart sank. "I see. I guess I'd better look into that flight home."

His mouth set in a grim line, he asked, "Is that what you want?"

"I should get back to California. I don't know how long they'll hold my job open."

"You have only been in Greece for a week. Surely a family bereavement justifies more time away than that."

"There's no point in my staying on the island alone. I've finished all I needed to do."

"You could come to Athens with me."

The words dropped like stones into the silence around them and she stared helplessly at him. He was inviting her to take another step forward in their relationship. Athens meant real life and he wanted to take her into it with him.

He said nothing, his expression as blank as an unendorsed check.

Her head told her to ignore the seductive attraction of such an invitation and get out while part of her heart was intact, but her heart told her it *already* belonged to the powerful man and to go for it.

She'd been ruled by her head all of her life and while she had a lifestyle far removed from anything resembling her mother's to show for it, she was also lonely. She'd wanted Sebastian for as long as she'd known him and the chance to do something about it stared her in the face.

To ignore it would be to forever shut a door her heart was screaming at her to walk through. "I'd like that."

His face transformed with a smile that she couldn't help returning.

"Then it shall be arranged."

The flight to Athens was a short one with no chance to communicate over the loud whir of the helicopter blades. Not that she would have interrupted Sebastian's intent study of documents from his briefcase even if she'd been wearing a communication headset. They were returning to Athens because he had no choice and that meant he needed to focus on the problem at hand, not entertaining her.

And she didn't mind. Simply being in his company was something special.

When they arrived in Athens, the limo driver dropped Sebastian off in front of his building and then took her to an apartment in an exclusive suburb of the city.

The chauffeur disappeared with her luggage and a middle-aged Greek woman offered her refreshments. Rachel refused, more interested in exploring Sebastian's sanctuary than anything else. The housekeeper nodded and returned to whatever she'd been doing when Rachel arrived.

His home was big and beautifully decorated, the great room big enough to fit her entire California apartment in with room to spare. It had an eating area as large as any formal dining room, a living area with a huge plasma screen television and a large corner of the room dedicated to reading with ceiling high bookcases and matching reading chairs.

All the furniture had a rather traditional feel; it and the accents were all done in smooth dark woods. His interior decorator liked neutral tones with splashes of color, which fit the vibrant man's personality rather well.

Inappropriate and no doubt misplaced jealousy had her wondering how well the designer knew her client. It was not even a fair thought, much less a rational one. There was nothing to say that Sebastian's designer had not been a man and absolutely no indication that the relationship had been anything but a professional one.

Nothing but Sebastian's reputation for dating beautiful career women while getting serious about none of them.

The possessive feelings coursing through Rachel were not unfamiliar and had been another reason why she had spent the last few years in the States. Living far away from Greece, she had not been forced to watch Sebastian with other women.

She walked into the first bedroom off the hall wondering how wise she'd been to come to Athens with a man who was unashamedly commitment phobic. Even if he *hadn't* despised her mother, he was hardly a sure thing in the emotional department.

The room she'd walked into was a fully furnished guest bedroom, but there was no sign of her luggage.

The next room had been converted into a home office complete with computer, printer, fax machine and a three-line telephone system. She didn't think he'd mind her using the computer to check her E-mail, so she powered it up, her chaotic thoughts still whirling around her decision to accompany Sebastian rather than fly home.

There was so little chance of a future for them that it was practically nonexistent. However, the feelings she had for him demanded she not walk away even if their chance at a future together had worse odds than winning the jackpot in California's state lottery.

She loved him.

She couldn't deny it. No other reason explained her inexplicable decision to stay on the island and to come with him to Athens knowing how little interest he had in a long-term relationship.

It was horribly ironic that she'd fallen in love with the one man programmed by her mother's behavior to steer clear of any woman from the Long family. But there *were* lottery winners and maybe she could be a winner at love too.

It took only a moment to check her E-mail via her server's Web site once the computer came online. There were several messages. So many in fact, that she almost deleted one from a friend of her mother's in a wholesale clearing of junk mail from her in-box. She stopped herself just in time and clicked on the message, expecting an expression of sympathy of her recent loss.

Instead, the E-mail was a barely coherent diatribe about Matthias Demakis and his threat to divorce

Andrea. It was only then that Rachel realized the message had been written the same day as the accident. She hadn't received it before she left and now wished she'd deleted it with the junk mail.

Apparently Matthias had gotten fed up with his wife's outrageous behavior and told her that he intended to divorce her, settling a small alimony stipend on her. Nothing like enough to make it possible for her to continue with her current decadent lifestyle. Her mother's friend believed Rachel should come to Greece and *stand beside Andrea in her time of need.*

The thought was a nauseating one.

The very suggestion she stand by her mother's side in such a scenario was obscene. The additional suggestion by her mother's friend that it was in Rachel's own best interest was just as appalling. She'd never considered Matthias Demakis a meal ticket and hated the fact that anyone would assume she did simply because she was Andrea's daughter. She would never have countenanced a bid for more money by Andrea from a man who had already paid far too much in his marriage to her.

The rest of her E-mails were innocuous and she finished going through them in very little time.

Afterward, she continued her exploring. Across the hall, she found Sebastian's bedroom. It was ultra-masculine and she could almost feel his presence amid the chocolate brown and vanilla decor. She spent several minutes just soaking in the reality of being inside his most private sanctuary.

She found her cases in the next room down the hall. The furnishings were decidedly feminine. Pale blue and peach with whitewashed wood made a departure from the other rooms in the apartment. Had he had the room designed for his lovers' comfort?

But no, she couldn't imagine him planning to have female guests overnight that were not intending to share his bed. Perhaps he'd had it decorated for his mother's visits. That was much more in keeping with his character.

The fact that he'd had her things put in the room indicated his willingness to respect her right to choose if and when they began a physical relationship. She appreciated Sebastian not assuming she would sleep with him immediately. However, she knew that if she stayed in his apartment for any length of time, it would not be sleeping in the double size bed in the beautiful guest room.

Sebastian rubbed his eyes and leaned back in his desk chair.

It had been a long day, with one draining meeting after another. The Chinese business contacts that had shown up unexpectedly had required careful handling and a tremendous focus on what was being said in each of their get-togethers. It had taken nearly half of the day for him to discern their objective in coming and the rest of the day making sure they did not achieve something not in his company's best interest.

The thought of going home to his apartment and seeing Rachel was very tempting, but he forced himself to go through his in-basket of personal correspondence before leaving. There were only a few letters, but some of them were over a week old.

He'd been gone for a lot longer than he'd originally planned when he'd flown to the island to take charge after his great-uncle's death. He'd taken care of business easily, but had told his secretary to hold off forwarding personal correspondence because he'd expected to be back sooner and he'd never rescinded that order.

Why, even though he'd been gone longer than expected?

Because he'd been focused on the confusing woman waiting in his apartment and he hadn't even thought of it.

He'd called her twice that afternoon, just like a lovesick boy. She'd responded like she was really happy to hear from him and was probably hearing wedding bells in her head.

He had no one to blame but himself. He shouldn't encourage her to think their relationship was out of the norm for him because he was not ready for marriage and emotional entanglement was right off his list of things to do for the next century.

He'd come much too close to going that direction once already to a woman a lot like Andrea Demakis, but he'd wised up in time and had paid in experience not alimony for his stupidity. He'd determined then not to let a woman get the upper hand in his life and his uncle's marriage had only reinforced that belief.

He didn't want to get married.

He sure as hell wasn't about to fall in love.

He picked up a letter that looked like it was addressed in Matthias's hand. He must be more tired than he thought. The return address was smudged, but it…

No it couldn't be.

It was.

The letter had been written by his great-uncle before his death, no doubt about it. The envelope was thick and Sebastian hesitated to open it. He didn't want to read something that would add to his ambivalent feelings about Rachel. He hated any sort of confusion and that seemed to be the vast majority of what he felt in relation to her.

But he was a man, not a spineless wimp, so he

slit the envelope marked personal and pulled out the several page letter. A half an hour later, the pages of the letter in an untidy heap in front of him on the desk, he sat in stunned silence, trying to digest what he'd read.

His uncle had wised up to his younger wife, but too late.

Not only had Matthias acknowledged what a horrible mistake he'd made in marrying Andrea, but he had written that he was concerned that if his mercenary wife thought she stood to gain by his death, he would not live very long. He had therefore changed his will to disinherit his wife completely.

The admission of such a mistake in judgment, not to mention the necessity of taking such action, would have been devastating to the old man's Greek pride and reading the words had made Sebastian physically ill.

Matthias had informed Andrea of the change in his will as well and his intention to divorce her. No wonder she'd gone so completely off the rails. She'd had nothing to lose anymore and a vindictive streak a mile wide. Realizing this, Matthias had written the letter to Sebastian so that in the event he did die before he got a divorce, his nephew would know that as far as he was concerned Andrea had no claim to the care given a widow within the family.

He stared down at the letter, the sick feeling in his stomach tightening into a knot of tension.

Had Andrea told her daughter their sugar daddy intended to evict them from his life? Had Rachel been angry, prepared to conspire with Andrea to get the biggest divorce settlement possible?

His teeth gritted as he rejected the thought.

Rachel was not anything like her mother. Hadn't she shown that to him in numerous ways already?

His rational mind reminded him that his uncle had been deceived by Andrea's false impression of innocence. Was Sebastian just as foolish in his dealing with a Long woman? Matthias had written that he'd married Andrea in order to protect her and had only later realized that far from being prey to the vagaries of life, Andrea had been predator through and through.

She'd convinced him that she'd had a traumatizing experience with a man and had played up to Matthias's protective instincts. It was only after the marriage that he'd realized far from being a victim, his wife was addicted to sex, not to mention alcohol and other substances that left her less than rational in her dealing with others.

But Rachel wasn't like that. She never drank. She didn't flirt and she didn't lie. She told the truth even when it embarrassed her. She wanted Sebastian, but she'd made no attempt to use sex to manipulate him.

She was perhaps one of the few totally honest women of his acquaintance.

Realizing that made him all the more eager to get home to her.

"What is that incredible smell?"

Rachel spun away from the stove where she had been adding the last minute spices to a pan of simmering curry chicken and landed smack against the immovable wall that was Sebastian.

His hands clamped on her arms before she could move away and his head lowered until his lips were almost touching hers. "Now this is the way a man likes to be greeted after a trying day."

Then his mouth finished its descent, slanting over hers with lazy affection. The scent of his expensive aftershave still clung to him from the morning, but it mixed with the smell of his skin to turn her bones to a jelly-like substance not intended to support her body in a vertical position.

Sagging against him, she clung to his shoulders, glad for his still firm grip on her arms. She had no defenses left against him and her body was making emphatic statements of desire in secret, tender places.

He must have had a glass of ouzo recently, she thought dizzily, the licorice flavor permeating her taste buds as his tongue penetrated her mouth. She loved his taste, his scent and the feel of his hard body against hers. Each of her senses was filled to overflowing with his presence.

Time ceased to mean anything and firm, masculine lips molded her own in one drugging kiss after another. His hands moved from her arms to her back, pressing her already pliant body into his firmness.

Something buzzed in the background, but she couldn't think what it was, and honestly didn't care.

However, Sebastian pulled his lips from hers, causing her to moan in protest and try to catch his mouth again with hungry lips.

He kissed her once, firmly, and then set her away from him. "Something is done, I think."

"Wh-what?" She couldn't think of anything but him, didn't want to look anywhere but at his beloved face.

"Dinner, *pethi mou.*" He turned her around to face the stove.

And her mind kicked into gear. *The curry.* She scrambled to turn off burners and pull the caramel flan she'd made for dessert from the oven. Nothing looked burned and she breathed out a sigh of relief.

"I told my housekeeper to inform you of my intention to eat out tonight."

Was that a criticism that she'd decided to cook?

She could not tell from his voice and was too busy removing the flan cups from the still simmering water to look at him. "You sounded tired the last time I spoke to you on the phone. I thought eating in would be more relaxing."

"*You* did not have to cook."

She turned to face him, biting her lower lip. "I'm sorry if I've overstepped the mark."

His shook his head, his expression wry. "You did not overstep, but you have surprised me."

"Good. That was the whole idea." She smiled at him. "I hope you like curry."

"I love it."

She'd thought that might be the case when she'd found pretty much all the ingredients she needed already stocked in the kitchen's large pantry.

He took a shower while she put the food on the table.

He joined her, wearing a pair of jeans and a

ribbed cotton shirt and looking like an advertisement for *Men's Fitness Magazine.* It was all she could do not to drool.

"I've never had a woman cook for me before." He surveyed the serving dishes filled with rice, chicken curry and spicy grilled vegetables. "It is a novel experience."

She started serving the food. "Good novel, or bad novel?"

"Definitely good. It makes me feel indulged." He reached out and touched her, his fingertips trailing down her arm, leaving shivery goose bumps behind. "I am usually the one doing the pampering."

She didn't like the reminder he had more pillow friends than silk ties, *and* it made her insecure.

She arranged the food on her plate with no desire to taste any of it and refused to meet his eyes. "I'm sure the other women in your life are far too sophisticated to enjoy a meal at home and an old movie on the television afterward."

She must seem so gauche to him. She knew the

women in his world didn't do the domestic bit, so why had she?

Because she liked to and her newly acknowledged love had demanded an expression.

When he'd called that afternoon to tell her he would be later than expected, he'd sounded exhausted, discouraged even. She had wanted to do something to help, but what was the point?

He had a housekeeper who could cook for him if he wanted to eat in. She would have spent the afternoon better occupied in an attempt to improve her image than acquainting herself with his kitchen.

"So is that what is on offer for later?"

"What?" Her head jolted up and she met his slate gaze, having lost the train of the conversation with her mental rambling.

"A movie."

"If you like."

He smiled and some of the tension inside her dissipated. "I like."

He took a bite of his dinner with every evidence of enjoyment and she followed suit, appreciating the burst of spicy sensation from the curry.

"How did you know I liked classic movies?" he asked a few minutes later.

"I didn't, but I'm glad you do." Or was he just trying to be kind? "Look, we don't have to watch it if you don't want to. This scene must seem pretty tame to you."

She indicated the table and her own less than perfectly coifed appearance. Her knee length khaki straight skirt and casual knit top would have been perfect for an evening at home in California, but were too sloppy for dinner with a man like Sebastian, she now appreciated.

Oh, well. She could hardly run into her room and change without looking like an idiot.

Sebastian had stopped eating and was looking at her.

She paused with her fork midway to her mouth. "What?"

"I like it."

"You like it?" She really wasn't grasping the conversation tonight.

"I enjoy being pampered. I like that you did all this for me and I like the idea of spending a couple of hours with you cuddled against me while we watch a movie."

"I don't fit in your world very well, Sebastian." She'd never fit in her mother's either. She wasn't the rich and famous type.

"Did I not just say I liked all this?" He looked confused.

"Yes, but you're simply being kind."

"I'm being honest." He frowned at her. "Do not spoil a special night doubting my sincerity."

Her breath caught in her throat. "Special?"

"Yes. Special. Believe it or not, the effort you made here is very special to me. *I like it,*" he stressed again.

Finally, she let herself believe him. "I'm glad. I wanted you to feel spoiled, but it didn't occur to me until you'd gotten home that you could have had your housekeeper cook you a meal if you wanted to stay home."

"But you did it because you wanted me to relax. Because you cared."

And it occurred to her that sophisticated, or not, she'd tapped into a real well of pleasure as far as her tycoon companion was concerned. He really did appreciate the personal touch. She beamed at him.

"And the night, it is not over. This wonderful dinner is only the beginning."

She swallowed hastily at the look in his eyes. She didn't think he was referring to the movie. If he meant what she suspected he meant, she would not deny him. She couldn't.

She loved him and if she were ever going to make love with a man, it would be Sebastian Kouros.

She licked suddenly dry lips and forced herself to say what needed to be said. "Tonight can be as special as you want it to be."

Recognition and desire flared in his eyes before a pained expression came over his features. "I want you, but I am not promising marriage here."

If he had one more ounce of tactlessness and one less of romantic idealism, he would be so basic, he wouldn't even have a rung on the evolutionary ladder. He was telling her he appreciated what she'd done tonight, would probably like even better the use of her body, but none of it altered the truth between them.

They had no future.

"I never thought you were. How could you? I'm Andrea's daughter and the last thing your family needs is a constant reminder of the pain she brought you all."

He opened his mouth to speak again, but she jumped up from the table. She'd had enough of this conversation. "Let me get dessert."

One more minute in his company right now and she would end up telling him to call one of his sophisticated women friends as commitment phobic as he was to make his night *special*.

"Rachel."

She didn't turn around. "I'll be right back."

"I didn't say it to hurt you, but it wouldn't be fair to take you to my bed without spelling out the terms."

"Of course." But it hurt just the same and she could no more help that than he could help not loving her.

Sebastian watched Rachel disappear through the door to the kitchen, frustration knotting his insides.

Could he have handled that any worse?

He had made her coming to his bed sound like a meaningless encounter between two people intent on scratching a sexual itch. It was nothing like that. He did not love her, could not marry her, but he desired her with a multilayered intensity he'd never known with another woman.

That's what he should have said, not the tactless spiel about not expecting a marriage proposal afterward.

When she came back in with the dessert, she gave him no opportunity to rectify his error, keeping up an animated flow of conversation about the movie they were going to watch, how kind his housekeeper had been to give up her kitchen and how much Rachel loved the decor in his apartment.

She'd given him an odd look when he'd told her the man's name who had designed it, but had not asked about him. She was too busy changing the subject to something equally impersonal, but when she moved as if to sit in a chair instead of next to him on the sofa to watch the movie, he'd had enough.

His hand snaked out and grabbed her. "You're supposed to cuddle next to me, remember?"

Her mouth, which had been mobile for the past twenty minutes, clamped shut.

"It is part of the special night you planned for me."

Instead of arguing like he expected, would even have welcomed, because it would have given him a chance to clear the air, she nodded jerkily.

He pulled her onto the sofa with him, before pushing the volume button on the remote control. Old movie music filled the room as he tugged her into a reclining position beside him. He couldn't help himself, but he wondered why she didn't fight it. She wasn't happy with him.

Despite her false front of bright chatter, he had no problem discerning that truth.

She gasped as they made body contact and he settled one arm around her waist. He looked down to find her eyes wide and her bow lips parted in surprise.

"This is called cuddling." He curled her against him as close as they could get with their clothes on.

At the feel of her warm soft body, he forgot his intention to force a confrontation and simply took what was on offer.

Maybe she didn't mind the fact that he wasn't planning on a happily ever after with her. Maybe he'd mistaken her anger.

He squeezed her waist. "Lay your head on my shoulder and relax."

Letting her head rest against him, her hand settled like a shy butterfly on his chest.

"Comfortable?" he asked, wondering how long he would last without touching her.

CHAPTER FIVE

SHE said nothing in reply to his question and he lasted one scene and two sighs from the woman beside him before his free hand went looking for bare skin beneath her loose top.

She sucked in a breath that seemed to suspend in her chest as his fingers met silky, smooth flesh just above the waistband of her skirt.

He let his hand rest there throughout the next scene, not moving, merely establishing his possession. Her fingers fluttered against his chest and embarked on a tentative exploration that made his heart accelerate into the danger zone.

"You are playing with fire," he warned her, still not ready to credit her willingness to be intimate with a man who had handled her offer of herself so badly.

"Are you saying I can make you burn?" The words should have been said with feminine seduction, instead she sounded shocked by the concept.

"*Ne*. Yes." He shuddered as one gentle fingertip brushed a hard nipple. "With you, I feel like Mount Vesuvius."

"Ready to explode?" she asked with a catch in her voice.

"Hot as the core of the earth itself."

"That's nice," she sighed against him, her hand continuing its tormenting exploration that was not enough.

Without taking his eyes off the television, he began to gently brush back and forth with his thumb against the indentation of her waist. Her fingers contracted on his chest, kneading him like a kitten.

"I am not *nice, pethi mou*." Such a tame word would never describe what he was intent on making her feel.

"No, you aren't." Something besides passion laced her voice, but he was too turned on to wonder what. "However, you *are* extremely sexy."

His laughter was harsh with want.

A kiss as soft as down brushed against his chest and he felt an unknown twinge in the region of his heart. It made him determined to get to her as deeply as she got to him.

He allowed his thumb to move higher up her torso with each caress, but always stopped shy of the generous and tempting curve of her breast.

Her small, feminine moan was music to his ears. Then she said his name in a long drawn out hiss and arched against him.

"What is it?" he asked, knowing exactly what she wanted.

"I need…"

He let his thumb rest just below the line of her bra. "*What* do you need?"

"You, Sebastian." Her head came up and she met his gaze, her green eyes dark with the depth of her emotion and he began to believe in something he had dismissed as fairy tale years ago. "I need *you*."

The uncontrolled passion and sincerity in her voice, the expression in her beautiful eyes combined to shatter his self-control. She wanted *him,* not his money, not even a wedding ring. *Just him.*

Had any woman ever wanted him only for himself? His ego wanted to say *yes,* but his bank account guaranteed he could not with certainty.

Rachel was different and the rage of his arousal reflected his body's reaction to that truth. He could not doubt her. She came to him without any promises, without any conditions.

And he would make sure she did not regret that choice.

Without any warning, Rachel found herself on her back, a sexually voracious male vibrating with his need to possess above her. A position that had caused her only terror in the past turned her on to the point of recklessness now and she tore at his shirt, yanking it from the waistband of his pants.

His big body convulsed when her hands encountered hot, hair roughened skin.

"You like that," she said with helpless wonder.

His powerful muscles tense and bulging, he hissed, *"Yes."*

It was incredible, unbelievable even, that she could affect him this way. The knowledge sent her fingers on a tactile exploration that covered every centimeter of his naked torso that she could reach.

He made guttural sounds deep in his throat and then reared up to tear his shirt all the way off, exposing gleaming, hard masculine planes to her eyes. Was it fair that any man should be so utterly, devastatingly gorgeous? Her eyes devoured him even as her hands reached out to press against the body giving her vision so much pleasure.

He reached for the hem of her knit top. "This goes too."

She waited to feel the fear the thought of being naked with a man would have brought before, but it did not come and grinned at him with unashamed triumph. "Yes!"

She helped him remove her shirt with hands that fumbled in their haste and he laughed once when they got their fingers tangled.

She'd been craving this closeness with him

since the night on the beach and now she *knew* it would be all right. Her mind splintered as his hands took possession of her naked skin. Her nipples ached to feel his touch, but he touched her everywhere else instead. He caressed her stomach, smoothed his warm hands down her arms, then up along her sides.

She shook with need, she moaned, but she had just enough mental capacity left to grit her teeth against begging.

It did no good. When his tormenting fingers strayed onto her breasts, but only drew circles around where she most needed his touch, her jaw unlocked and she shouted in raw demand, *"Touch me there."*

His steel gray eyes burned her with sensual promise as his fingertips finally trespassed onto turgid peaks, stinging with need. She bowed up toward him, offering him her breasts which he accepted willingly, peeling away her bra to expose her completely to his gaze and touch.

He leaned down and kissed each tip, licking it like a cat before raising his head to meet her gaze. Her eyes were wet with a surfeit of emotion and his name came out on a broken sob. He touched her again, giving her so much pleasure, she shook with the feelings he evoked.

A feverish daze came over her so that she was aware of only the affect his expert caresses had on her body. Somehow he removed the rest of their clothes and then it was full body contact, heart to heart, skin to skin, moist feminine welcome against hard male flesh.

It was so alien and yet more wonderful than anything she'd ever known.

That other time, that man had not even undressed all the way, but Sebastian wanted more than sexual release from her body, he wanted to be *intimate* with her. Every word out of his mouth, every movement by his body told her this.

Legs slid against legs. Torsos meshed. His mouth came down on hers, his lips demanding all she had to give and she willingly gave it. He crushed her highly sensitized breasts into the thick mat of hair on his chest, pulling her body toward him with ardent hands while thrusting his pelvis against her.

His tongue thrust into her mouth, emulating a mating dance she had thought she would never want to engage in. Well, she wanted now. Oh, how she wanted.

Her legs separated in an age-old invitation and he rubbed his hard flesh against her swollen flesh. Sensation zinged through her feminine center. His mouth broke from hers to trail sexy kisses down her throat.

"I have to taste you," he said against the skin of her neck.

She couldn't make sense of his words. Wasn't he tasting her already?

He nibbled at the base of her neck and she shivered. "Oh, Sebastian, oh..." She couldn't get anything else out and kept saying his name over and over again.

He didn't stop the tasting at her neck, but moved to her breasts, giving her love bites on the resilient flesh that sent sensation arcing through her. When he started suckling her tender peaks, the feeling went straight to her womb and she cried out with the cataclysmic pleasure of it.

Despite her attempt with frantic hands to keep him at her breast, he moved down her body, stopping at her belly button to submit it to a sensual torture she would never have believed possible. When he pressed her legs farther apart, she let him without thought to the consequences, but when his head lowered and he kissed her in the most intimate way possible, shock at the unexpected sensation made her try to buck him off.

He raised his head, his expression that of a jungle animal thwarted of its prey. "Do you not want the pleasure I can give you?"

How could she answer that? "I've never…"

His brows rose. "Ah, a man has not tasted your sweet nectar before?"

"No," she croaked.

His eyes questioned her.

"Never," she affirmed.

Definite male satisfaction glowed in his molten gaze. "I want to taste you, Rachel. Let me."

It sounded more like a demand than a request for permission, but he had stopped and she could not deny him. Not when telling him *no* meant

stifling desires consuming her with unquench-
able flames.

"Yes."

His smile made her shiver even as her body
melted under another intimate kiss from his too
knowing mouth.

Sebastian savored the essence of Rachel with a
consuming need to imprint himself on her, to make
her know she was his. Her excitement was sweet
and her scent so feminine it drove him wild. No
woman had tantalized him like this one, had made
him want her until he could taste her mouth in his
dreams and feel her body when he closed his eyes.

He brushed his thumb against her pleasure spot
while taking possession of slick, swollen
feminine flesh with his tongue.

She gave no warning before her body went
rigid in ecstasy and a scream of fulfillment burst
from her lips. It continued to echo in his mind
long after the only sounds coming from her
mouth were tiny whimpers of residual pleasure.

Her body was still shaking with aftershocks

when he came up over her and positioned his hardness at the entrance to her hot velvet depths.

He kissed her rosebud lips, reveling in their taste as much as he had enjoyed the sweet core of her.

"I want you," he rasped.

Her eyes fluttered open, the expression in them soft and full of an emotion that impacted him to the depths of his soul. "I want you too, but please…"

"Please, what?" He could barely get the words out, his need was so great.

"Don't hurt me."

Ardor ebbed, though it did not leave completely as he considered her reasons for making such a request. "You *believe* I will hurt you?"

"No, but…"

Her innocent reactions, the surprised way she responded to his every touch, her instant rejection of his mouth on her…they all added up to a truth he could barely credit. "You are a virgin?"

"Yes."

"But you are twenty-three." He could not help the shocked words from leaving his mouth.

"I have never felt this way about another man."

He looked down at her, his heart pounding in his chest and he believed her. "Then you do me a great honor."

He bent and lifted her into his arms.

Her eyes filled with vulnerable appeal and an unstoppable wave of tenderness swept over him. Never before had it been so important to ensure his partner's pleasure and well-being, but he was determined to make her first time one she would remember always.

He bent down and kissed her with lips gentled by the feelings coursing through him. "It will be perfect, *agape mou*. I promise you."

She reached up and returned his kiss, hers full of trust and a surrender as ancient as Adam and Eve. "I believe you, my love."

Did she know what she had called him?

He looked into her beautiful green eyes, glazed with passion and he did not think so, but just because she was not conscious of the words did not mean she did not feel them. He had blinded himself to her feelings because he thought he had to, but Rachel was as far removed from the woman who had given her birth as a nun from a prostitute.

He forced himself to take the time to arouse her all over again, to bring her to the brink of climax before carefully beginning to ease himself into her body. As silken tissues stretched around him, an incontrovertible truth assailed him.

Nothing but marriage would do.

The thought of another man doing to her what he was about to do was intolerable.

"You are mine," he growled as her tightness allowed him to gain only the beginning of entry.

Love glazed eyes stared back at him and she nodded. "Yes. I'm yours. I always have been."

Her mass of silky brown hair, long since fallen out of its conservative style, spread around her on the sofa cushions like a pagan goddess of old.

It took more self-control than he thought he had, but he eased into her slow inch by slow inch. The farther he sank into her body, the more fractured his thoughts became. The lack of any impediment to his progress registered only on the periphery of his mind as his own passion took control of him.

He made love to her in a state of mind-numbed need, the pleasure blasting through him greater than anything he had ever known.

She moved under him, the noises coming from her throat desperate and carnal. Again, she gave no warning, but climaxed beneath him with powerful contractions in the swollen tissues surrounding his needy flesh. And he joined her, the world going black around the edges for several incredible seconds.

When he came fully to himself, he was collapsed on top of her. He felt weak in a way he had sworn he would never allow himself to experience.

She was crying, soft, silent tears.

"Did I hurt you?" His gut twisted in agony at the prospect.

She shook her head causing more moisture to leak out of her eyes. "It was the most incredible experience of my life. Thank you."

He carefully pulled himself back from her, frowning at her sucked in breath as he withdrew completely. "You are all right?"

"Oh, yes. It's just so different. Every little movement sets off earthquake tremors inside me." She said it apologetically, but he shook his head in wonder.

Did she have no idea how special a lover she was?

She was asleep before her head even rested against the pillow. He climbed in beside her, physically replete as he'd never been before.

He woke her in the night twice and both times she gave herself to him with delightful abandon.

Sebastian woke with a sense of having lost something important.

Himself.

Never before in his life had he experienced such intense need, such driven desire. Nor had he experienced the depth of emotional connection with another woman that he knew with Rachel. His body had possessed hers, but she had also possessed him and left him with a need he did not believe would ever be completely slaked.

A man was a fool to let any woman have this sort of power over him, but he was helpless to minimize his reaction to her.

The only redemption he could find in the situation was that their obsession was completely mutual.

She could not resist him.

Soft warmth cuddled against his side and sensual memories of the night before came flooding back, attesting to that. Rachel had participated in their lovemaking to the very depths of her being. She was an amazing lover, a woman like no other. Every man's dream.

A sense of disorientation assailed him as he remembered a line from his uncle's letter.

Matthias had said the same thing about Andrea, that she was *every man's dream in bed*. The old man had written that he had continued in his travesty of a marriage for so long, not only because of the desire Andrea elicited in him. He had also been addicted to the sexual response she gave him.

Addiction. The word was too close to Sebastian's feelings for Rachel to be comfortable.

But he was not so enslaved to his libido that he would allow a woman to destroy his pride and trample his masculine dignity because she was good in bed.

Wouldn't you?, a tormenting voice prompted in his head.

His thoughts in turmoil, he let his gaze settle on the small woman sleeping beside him. He could not see her face because it was covered in a cloud of brown silk, but the top swells of her breasts were revealed above the duvet and he could feel their softness against his skin. Sexual desire roared up hot and hungry and he had to bite down on the urge to touch her into wakefulness.

Addiction. Obsession. How different were they?

But was he addicted? He wanted, but he did not have to take. He could survive not making love. He was no slave to his passions.

Besides a virgin deserved some consideration.

That thought was a more effective checker to his tortuous want than any determination to prove his ability to control his libido. He did not want to hurt her, but thinking back to the night before, he could not remember hurting her at all. Not even the first time.

Memories began to niggle at him, impressions of the night before that he had been unable to assimilate in his rapture dazed mind. There hadn't been any blood.

A woman's virginity had to be carefully breached because it caused the rupture of a thin membrane of flesh inside her, the result of which was blood. But she hadn't bled. She also had not been sore. She had accommodated him with eager acceptance every time they made love.

She had told him she was a virgin, but the evidence was to the contrary.

The prospect that Rachel had lied to him about her innocence made his insides tighten in fury and pain until he was nauseous with it.

Hadn't Andrea suckered his uncle into believing she was far more innocent sexually than she really was?

Was Rachel set on ensnaring him just as her mother had ensnared Matthias?

She had let him make love to her even though he had clearly stated marriage was not on offer. Why?

A curse erupted from his throat as he remembered something else from the night before. They hadn't used anything for protection the night before. She had never even mentioned it, not when he'd clumsily told her he wanted her without strings or later when they made love. He dismissed as irrelevant the fact he had said nothing himself.

It was only one step further in his admittedly agitated thought process to decide that had been her plan all along. She hadn't asked for a commitment because she'd planned to trap him into one. Rachel had been even more devious than her mother, for he had never been fooled by Andrea.

Rachel had taken him in completely.

When he thought of his decision the night before to marry her, the sickness inside him grew.

She was a professional player of extraordinary skill.

Rachel came out of the bathroom wrapped in Sebastian's oversize robe. She'd woken up alone, but had tried not to be bothered by that fact. He was a businessman and had spent days away from his company. He would have a lot to catch up on. For all she knew, yesterday's reason for the urgently called meeting still existed.

She would not see it as a dismissal of her importance in his life. No man could make love as tenderly as he had to her and not feel anything but lust.

He'd been so gentle with her, and her heart swelled with the memory. As far as first times went, it had been ideal. Amazing. Beautiful. Wonderful. Her face creased in a goofy smile as the superlatives rolled through her mind.

Sebastian Kouros was the perfect lover.

And she didn't want their relationship to end, but she had asked for no promises and he had offered none. If she told him the truth, about her feelings and her past, would it make any difference?

He had to know she was nothing like her mother now. Rachel had come to Sebastian a virgin. She did not sleep around and she loved him. She was almost positive she'd told him so at one point during their lovemaking. Dared she repeat the words in the cold light of day?

Could she stand the definite cost she would pay for her cowardice if she did not? Sebastian would let her go back to America believing she didn't want anything more than an intense sexual encounter, when in fact, she wanted it all.

She doubted he loved her, but he felt something deeper for her than mere lust. Was it enough to build a relationship on? Would he even want to?

She would not know unless she came clean with him.

Besides, love was honest. It didn't hide behind pride or a fear of the past.

There was so much she hadn't told him about her past, things that would let him know she was not and would never be like her mother. After her experience as a teenager, she had rejected Andrea's way of life completely and Sebastian was bound to believe her when she told him. He was a smart man. He would understand.

He would believe she truly loved him when he realized she had been able to let *him* make love to her after that trauma.

She got up and headed for the door, ready to tell him everything, only to be brought up short when Sebastian walked into the room, his expression grim.

"Are you all right?" she asked, wondering if another time would be better to discuss their feelings and their future.

He didn't look very receptive.

Almost immediately, she chastised herself for being a coward. Sebastian owned a multinational corporation. There would always be events that were bound to cause a deterioration in his mood. She had to believe her emotions and his could rise above that.

"I am fine." His gaze flicked over her, a strange light in his gray eyes. "Did you sleep well?"

"Yes." She took a deep breath. "Sebastian, there is something I need to tell you."

"Is there?" He didn't *sound* all that receptive either.

"Yes. Please, will you hear me out?"

His lips twisted in a parody of a smile. "I believe I already know what it is."

"No, I don't think you do." He was more intelligent than any man she'd ever known, but even Sebastian wasn't a mind reader.

"It is related to the matter of your virginity," he guessed, his voice curiously flat.

Shocked, she stared at him, incapable of speech for several seconds. How could he know?

"Andrea told you?" she asked in disbelief, but unable to come up with another scenario that made any sense.

"Yes. I figured it out through your mother."

That was an extremely odd way of putting it. "Sebastian, I'm talking about what happened to me when I was sixteen. Do you know about that?"

He paled and bitter anger crossed his features before he wiped them of all expression once again. "You are about to tell me you had a traumatic experience with a man, no?"

She nodded, but found it was harder to talk about than she had expected.

She sat down on the edge of the bed, her knees feeling wobbly. "I can't believe she told you. She made me swear never to say a word."

"And now you are going to tell me that you did not believe you could respond to a man, but I have brought out your womanly passion." The total lack of emotion in his voice bothered her.

"Yes," she said nervously. She wished she could tell what he was thinking.

"*Ne*, yes, I am not easily fooled."

He was talking about it all so dispassionately and yet, perhaps that was how he was dealing with it. If he cared about her and after last night, she believed he did, he would be furious about what had happened to her. He was a traditional Greek man, possessive and protective. This was probably as hard for him as it was for her to discuss.

"I know you very well." His words confirmed her hopes.

She nodded, choking on emotion. "Yes, you do and maybe that is one of the reasons that I love you so very much."

His face contorted as if in pain and he spun away from her. "Tell me something, Rachel."

She hadn't expected him to match her declaration. Men like Sebastian didn't give in to their feelings very easily, but she hadn't thought he would dismiss her completely either.

Perhaps his turning away did not signify that. "Anything."

"You are aware Matthias had denounced Andrea and planned to divorce her?"

She didn't know what that had to do with her and Sebastian, but she sighed. "One of her friends E-mailed me with the news."

He whipped back around to face her, the ice in his eyes sending shivers down her spine. "So, this knowledge is what prompted the big seduction scene last night."

"What big seduction scene?" Nothing was going the way she had anticipated and he was confusing her.

"The dinner, your willingness to be close to me even after I told you I would not offer marriage. It all adds up now. You came to Greece knowing your mother had been cut off. You didn't want your meal ticket to end so you made a play for another rich man."

"What are you talking about?"

He sliced the air with his hand. "I am talking about you, the *innocent virgin*," he said the words with major scorn, "allowing yourself to have sex for the *first time* with me, the meal ticket."

She couldn't believe he was saying these things, more and more horror filling her with each passing word until she was as cold as his eyes. She wrapped her arms around herself, but it did not help a cold that had started in her heart and was radiating outward.

"You believe I made love with you because I was looking for money?" She wanted to scream the words, but they came out a harsh whisper instead. *You think I came to Greece for my mother's funeral intent on seducing you?"*

Not only was the suggestion a sick one, it also indicated a colossal ego she'd give anything to deflate until he felt as empty as she did right now.

"You knew about the divorce."

"I didn't know before I came to Greece. I found out yesterday."

"Who told you, a Mina bird?" he asked deridingly.

She tried to explain about the E-mail, about how it had been waiting in her in-box with all the others, but he simply stood there in stone-faced rejection as if her words impacted him not one iota.

"You expect me to believe Andrea did not call you in a temper and tell you the truth, but that one of her friends sent you an E-mail you conveniently received posthumously?"

It did sound unlikely, but not impossible and

if he respected and trusted her at all, he would not deride it as a quickly composed lie.

"No, I don't expect you to believe it, but it's the truth," she uttered, defeat sinking into her bones as her dreams shattered around her.

CHAPTER SIX

"YOU said you knew me. If you did, you'd know how hard last night was for me after what happened to me when I was younger."

"That trick has been played too. It may have worked on Matthias, but it will not work on me."

Her mother had pretended to have a sexual trauma in her past? She would believe anything of her mother, she'd had a lifetime of her games but could not take in how Sebastian had changed from a warm and caring lover to a cold and heartless stranger.

How could everything have gone so wrong? "Last night was beautiful."

Something came and went in his eyes, but she didn't even try to figure out what. Her heart was dying inside of her.

"A beautiful bit of manipulation, you mean, but I am not my uncle and I will not be deceived by my libido into a relationship with a mercenary bitch."

She surged off the bed, the last insult one too many. "Don't you dare call me names!"

"Does the truth hurt?" he taunted.

"The truth? What would you know about the truth? You're as deceived as Matthias ever was." He believed lies about her, only they were lies of his own making. She'd never once misled him. "I'm not like my mother. I came to you a virgin, for heaven's sake."

He looked as unconvinced as a heartless statue. "Your virginity was as false as your supposed love."

She shook her head, trying to clear it, trying to come to terms with his words. "You don't believe I was a virgin?"

"You've caught yourself in your own lies. You implied you were raped, but then say you are a virgin. Which is it?"

"I never had sex before." It was all she was

prepared to say at this point. She wasn't about to bare her most painful memory to him, not after all he'd said.

"You did not bleed."

And that was his incontrovertible proof she had sexual experience? *That she did not bleed?*

No, she hadn't. She'd bled at sixteen though, so much so that she'd been terrified she would die. Andrea had refused to take her to Emergency, had told her not to be a baby, that all women bled when their hymen broke.

She was bleeding again now. Inside where he could not see, her love was hemorrhaging to death and the pain was even worse than it had been that horrible day so long ago.

"I didn't demand marriage. I gave myself to you freely. Doesn't that count for anything?" She wasn't even trying to convince him anymore, she was simply pointing out the obvious.

"You sold yourself too cheaply."

Each word was like a slap in the face. She hadn't sold herself at all.

If he thought the act of lovemaking outside of

marriage had been a no-brainer for her, then he was pig-ignorant where she was concerned. She'd never accepted her mother's lifestyle as the right one to follow. She'd wanted a wedding night, a white gown and Prince Charming, but she'd settled for the prince without the trappings because she'd loved him so much.

And she'd hoped he would see her love for what it was, value the gift of her heart.

She'd been an idiot. A stupid, naive, idiot.

"Nothing else to say?" he asked, a tone in his voice she did not recognize.

She just shook her head, refusing to look at him again. Her heart hurt so much, she wondered if emotional pain could stop its beating as effectively as a heart attack.

He stood there for several seconds looking at her, the tension in him a palpable entity, but finally he spun on his heel and left the bedroom.

She sat, her heart turning to stone in her chest, her pain morphing into an impenetrable wall around emotions she would never risk giving in to again.

It was a long time before she was able to stand on legs that felt like rubber bands stretched unbearably taut, but she did. Then she dropped the robe from her shoulders, unable to bear the feel of anything belonging to him next to her skin. She walked naked from the bedroom, across the hall and into her own room and shut the door. Then she locked it.

Out of the corner of her eye, she had seen movement, but she refused to turn her head to see who it was. She didn't even care if it were one of his employees and they had seen her naked. Nothing mattered anymore.

The process of emotional decimation Andrea started so long ago had been completed in Sebastian's bedroom.

Rachel had been a fool to love such a monster.

The leaden weight in her chest told her she would not make such a mistake again. She was anesthetized against future pain because she could not feel anymore. Surprisingly, she wasn't even sad now. She was just…nothing. Numb.

And she was glad.

She had had her fill of pain.

She packed her cases. She pulled out the box of mementos she'd added to in the last week, a shell from the beach the day of their fishing trip, a flower Sebastian had picked her on one of their walks, simple things that did nothing but taunt her with her own emotional stupidity. Refusing to even look inside, she tossed it in the garbage can, then she called the airline with her ticket and agreed to come into the airport and wait stand-by for the next available flight. Next she called a taxi.

Thirty minutes later, she left the apartment. Sebastian's voice filtered through the study door as she passed, but she had no desire to stop and say, "Goodbye." Everything had been said and she could only hope she never saw the cynical bastard again.

"And how is your guest, son?"

Sebastian gripped the phone tightly and sucked in choking air at his mother's question. The last time he'd seen his *guest,* she had looked devastated.

He'd spent the last couple of hours trying to get her and last night off his mind, but it hadn't worked. Urgent company business could not keep his thoughts from her and his mother's question just served to bring everything to the forefront of his mind with blinding clarity.

His words, her reactions, assumptions that lost their power to convince in the chilled light of reality not overshadowed by gut clenching emotion.

God in Heaven, what have I done?

There was no answer from above, but his mother called his name across the phone line.

"Ne?"

"I asked how Rachel is doing."

"Not well."

"You had an argument?" his mother asked, managing to convey both censure and her belief it was his fault with four short words.

"She is just like her mother."

"You don't really believe that, do you?"

Things were shifting inside his head, but to admit he had been completely wrong would be to contemplate a hell of his own making. "What are the chances she would be different?"

"You are a fool if you believe this of her."

To be called a fool by his mother was not a pleasing experience and Sebastian gritted his teeth in frustration. "You are so certain. Tell me why."

"An hour in her company is enough to show that two people could not be more dissimilar. You have let your prejudice color your judgment."

He had thought that too, but then he'd convinced himself he was wrong. "Perhaps you have allowed your compassion to color yours."

His mother's sigh was long and full of parental disapproval. "She has spent the last several years living completely separate from Andrea. Not only did she insist on living in another country, away from her mother's influence, but Rachel stopped accepting support funds from Matthias when she graduated from university. If she were like Andrea, wouldn't she have been in Greece, participating in her mother's decadent lifestyle? At the very least she would have allowed Matthias to augment her income."

Cold that had been curling at the edges of his thoughts began to fill his being. "I did not know Matthias had ceased supporting her."

"But then you changed the subject every time her name was mentioned in the last few years."

He had wanted her and hearing about her had only exacerbated an ever-increasing ache.

"She lied to me," he said in a last-ditch effort to hold on to the protection of his assumptions.

"This I do not believe."

Goaded by the reproach in his mother's voice, he told her the truth. "Rachel said she was a virgin, but she wasn't. She was trying to trap me just like Andrea trapped Matthias."

His mother's gasp was followed by a moan of true Greek distress. "And how can you be so sure of this?"

Used to his parent's unquestioning approval, her continued certainty he was in the wrong made him angry. "How do you think?"

A word came out of his mother's mouth he'd never heard her utter before. "Do not tell me that you accused her of these things after making love with her."

"I will not be deceived like my uncle."

"No, you will merely deceive yourself. Oh, you foolish child."

Despite his annoyance at being called foolish yet again, his mouth twisted at the incongruity of being called a child at the age of thirty.

"On what evidence did you base your assumption she is not a virgin?"

"That is not something I will discuss with you."

"Who will you discuss it with then? If you can make the accusation, you can tell me your reasons for doing so."

"She did not bleed." Even though miles and phone lines separated them, he actually flushed with embarrassment after saying such a thing to his mother.

"So?"

"So, she wasn't innocent like she claimed and damn it, Mama, I would not have cared, but if she would lie to me about this, she would lie about other things."

"And on this reasoning you broke her heart?"

"I did not break her heart."

"You did not reject her?"

"I made her no promises to begin with."

"And she is the one you call a deceiver?" Suddenly, his mother went off into a tirade about idiotic and stubborn Greek men. She informed him that even a dinosaur like himself should realize not all women made it into adulthood with their hymen intact. The lack of blood was no evidence at all.

His mother was ashamed of him for taking Rachel's innocence outside of the bonds of marriage and then accusing her with trumped-up charges. She ended by telling him that he would deserve it if Rachel refused to ever speak to him again and she, Phillippa Kouros, would never attempt to match make for such an idiotic son again.

If she wanted grandchildren, she would have to wait for his brother to be ready to wed because she didn't want her grandchildren carrying such imprudent, cynical genes.

Sebastian's ears rang for several minutes after his mother hung up on him.

His mother was right. How could he have convinced himself of those things about Rachel? She had never in any way exhibited the least tendency to be like her mother and yet in true Greek vendetta fashion, he had held her accountable for her mother's sins.

The blood drained from his face as he remembered all the things he had said to her, the accusations he had made. He'd hurt her when she had given herself to him freely and the truth had been in her lovely, wounded eyes for him to see.

He had even convinced himself that making love without protection had been her fault when in fact, it had been his. He was the experienced one and wanting to be inside her more than he wanted to breathe, he hadn't even *thought* of safe sex.

His mother's words were nothing compared to the thoughts castigating him now.

A deep abyss loomed before him, dark, cold, and isolated. If he could not make it up to Rachel, he would fall into it.

Not looking forward to swallowing his words, he went to her room to find her, but when he reached it, it was empty.

Not only of Rachel, but of her things.

His stomach tightened into a knot and his breathing became erratic as he yanked open bureau drawers and closet doors, confirming what he knew to be true: she was gone.

His gaze skated around the room, looking for any sign of her, a note, anything and he noticed a decorative box in the trash bin. It looked like a memory keepsake box like his mother had on her bedroom dresser. She kept things that had belonged to his father in it.

What was it doing in Rachel's trash bin? She'd brought it all the way from the island, it was odd she would choose now to throw it away.

He picked it up and opened it without compunction. As his eyes registered what was inside, a feeling of dread swept through him. She had literally thrown him out of her life and every memory that accompanied him. Mementos from as far back as their first meeting nestled together in a carefully arranged assortment, all of it testament to feelings Rachel had had for him since the beginning.

Feelings he had ignored.

No, that wasn't quite true. He'd noticed her shy adoration and he'd played up to it sometimes, being kind to her because she'd drawn him like no other woman. Even when she'd been a mere seventeen years old. He had wanted her even then, but her innocence had screamed out at him, as had her reticence around men. She never swam when her mother's friends were around, though she'd gone swimming a few times with him.

She had avoided Andrea's parties when she lived on the island.

The sheer idiocy of his earlier convictions struck him anew. His only excuse was that he'd been going crazy since Matthias's death. His grief at losing a man who had been both a father figure and a business mentor to him had been intensified by the senselessness of the old man's death and grief at the thing his life had become since marriage to the bitch, Andrea.

Mixed with a need he had not wanted to feel for Rachel, but could no longer control, it had fried his brains into oblivion.

Rachel sat in the vinyl covered office chair, numbing disbelief paralyzing her vocal chords.

The doctor's no-nonsense expression offered no comfort in the face of such devastating news.

She'd come in to find out what was going on with her female hormones and she'd been slapped with this.

"It's not an uncommon condition. You would be surprised at how many people under the age of thirty have heart disease. Atrial fibrillation is the most common and one of the mildest forms."

Mild? She did not consider the risk of stroke or congestive heart failure mild, but perhaps it was all in a person's perspective. No doubt Dr. Pompella saw patients in much worse shape than Rachel quite frequently.

"Successful treatment of the hyperthyroidism that caused the arrhythmia in the first place could result in the disappearance of your atrial fibrillation."

"And if it doesn't, the treatment for that is to knock me out and stop my heart?" That didn't seem all that mild to her either.

Dr. Pompella nodded, her dark gaze impassive. "The risk involved is quite small."

"How small?"

"If the cardioversion is attempted without a regime of blood thinners beforehand, it could cause a stroke. However, after six weeks of warfarin treatment, the risk of stroke is almost nonexistent."

Did doctors get paid extra for talking over their patient's head? "So, how do we treat my thyroid condition?"

She was twenty-three years old and too darn young to have this sort of thing to deal with. Only, according to her doctor, an overactive thyroid was also quite common.

"You have the choice of treating it with medication, surgery or mild radiation therapy."

After explaining that the chances of long-term

success with medication therapy were less than thirty percent, Rachel asked about the radiation therapy. Swallowing a drink with radiation laced iodine sounded a lot easier than having surgery.

It was also painless, didn't have any lasting side effects, other than the desired one and was done completely out-patient. "However, you'll want to stay away from small children and refrain from hugging anyone else for seventy-two hours after drinking the treatment."

"I see." An issue she'd been trying to ignore for the last two months refused to be dismissed any longer. "What impact might this have on pregnancy?"

"Is there a possibility that you might be pregnant?"

"I don't know."

The doctor's eyes widened.

"I had my period a week after…" Her voice trailed off when she couldn't make herself give voice to what she and Sebastian had done. She took a deep breath and let it out. "It was light and I haven't had another period in two months."

"No morning sickness?"

"No."

"Are your breasts tender?"

"A little. I guess." She didn't go around touching her breasts except to wash them in the shower.

Had she instinctively been more careful of them lately? She thought maybe she had.

"There are a lot of reasons for a missed period besides pregnancy."

That's what she'd been telling herself. "I know. That's why I made the appointment for a physical."

She had certainly not expected to come in and be told she had a heart condition brought about by an overactive thyroid.

"Pregnancy would prevent the use of radiation therapy for your thyroid condition. If you have time, we can run a pregnancy test now, before making any further decisions."

"Yes."

An hour later, she sat in the same rose pink vinyl chair, feeling like her world had caved in on her. "I'm ten weeks pregnant?"

"That is correct." Dr. Pompella closed the manila folder in front of her. "We need to discuss options."

"Yes," but Rachel's attention wasn't focused on the doctor.

For the same two and a half months the baby had been growing inside her, she had been shut down emotionally, surviving in a cocoon of isolation into which no other person had been allowed any real access. Suddenly, another living being was in the cocoon with her and she couldn't separate herself. She was going to have a baby and that baby would be inside her defense mechanisms for the rest of her life.

"Is the father in the picture?"

Rachel's gaze refocused on the doctor. "No." An image of Sebastian tried to come forward in her mind and she slammed a mental door on it with a resounding clang. "He's not in my life at all."

"Ten weeks is not too far along to consider a termination." Dr. Pompella spoke without a shred of emotion.

Fierce protectiveness for the small life

growing inside her welled up in Rachel. "That is not an option."

The other woman's mouth set in a firm line. "You should at least consider it."

"No."

"I don't think you've considered all the angles to your situation. If you don't treat your hyperthyroidism, your heart arrhythmia will continue, putting you at risk for both stroke and heart attack. The medications that could treat the arrhythmia can have adverse side effects on pregnancy as well."

"Then I won't take them."

"Which leaves you with two potentially serious medical conditions going untreated for the next seven months."

"Aren't there any treatments available that are safe for pregnancy?"

"You could try beta-blockers, but taking an aggressive approach early in your condition is going to give you the best chance of complete recovery. And beta-blockers are not completely risk free," she stressed.

Rachel told the doctor she would consider alternatives and thanked her for her time, but went home determined not to return to Dr. Pompella.

Anyone who thought killing her baby was the answer to problems she didn't even have physical symptoms for was crazy.

She reasoned that she hadn't even known about the heart arrhythmia or hyperactive thyroid until she'd gone in for her physical, so neither could be all that bad.

She did her best to eat food healthy for both her heart and her baby, and managed a daily dose of light exercise. Working at a women's fitness center, that part was easy. She found an obstetrician and started taking prenatal vitamins as well. She felt physically better than she had at any time in her life and pushing the worry to the back of her mind, Rachel didn't bother to mention her heart arrhythmia to her OB.

If she still longed for Sebastian in the darkest hours of the night, she refused to give such craven feelings airtime in the light of day.

Her attitude of complacency about her heart

condition lasted until she woke up in an ambulance, headed toward Emergency after collapsing at work.

She was able to go home a few hours later, but the reality of her condition had well and truly sunk in.

She had to make sure her baby would be taken care of if something happened to her. The urge to call Sebastian had been growing daily in the two weeks since she discovered her pregnancy. She no longer loved him. How could she after all he had said to her? However, she would not allow her child to be deprived of its father as Rachel had been of hers.

It didn't matter that Sebastian thought she was a reincarnation of Andrea, or even that he would see the pregnancy as another trap. She wasn't trying to trap him and he would eventually figure that out. He loved his family and once he accepted that the baby was his, he would love it too. He would ensure their baby would never be alone, no matter what happened to Rachel.

She called Sebastian's office the next day.

His secretary offered to take a message because Sebastian was in a meeting.

When Rachel gave her name the secretary said, "Rachel Long?" as if she couldn't quite believe her ears.

"Yes, though if you're going to have him call me back at work, have him ask for Rachel Newman."

"Please, hold the line." The secretary sounded quite agitated. "I'll have Kyrios Kouros for you directly."

"Oh, no, that isn't necessary. He can call me back."

"I have strict instructions, Ms. Newman."

What instructions? She would have thought Sebastian would tell his secretary to refuse to take any call from her, not to interrupt him in an important meeting. She had barely a minute to consider the puzzle before his deep voice came across the phone line.

"Rachel?" His tone was oddly thick.

"Yes."

"Rachel *Newman* now?" he asked, a very odd inflection in his tone.

"Yes."

"I…I'm…"

He was silent so long, she thought the connection might have gone dead. "Sebastian?"

"*Ne,* yes." Again that thick voice. "I suppose congratulations are in order."

If he routinely offered congratulations in that tone of voice, he would not have very many friends.

"What for?" No way could he know about the baby.

"Your marriage."

What in the world was he talking about? "Are you crazy? I'm not married."

"You are not?"

"No."

Did he honestly believe she would go from him to another man that fast…and get *married?* She supposed he did, thinking she was a world-class slut and liar.

"Then what is this Rachel *Newman?*" Anger vibrated in his voice, confusing her further.

But she'd forgotten he didn't know about her

changing her last name. She told him about it now.

"We could find nothing and that explains it."

"What?"

"It is not important. You called me for a reason, *agape mou*. What is it?"

The phone connection must be fuzzy. She could have sworn he called her his love, but that was not possible. "I have something I need to tell you. Two things really."

"Tell me these things."

"I'm pregnant. I know you aren't going to believe the baby is yours until we can have tests, but I'm willing to have those." She'd made the decision not to allow her pride to get in the way of her baby's welfare before she'd ever picked up the phone to call him.

Again the silence.

"Sebastian?"

"I am here."

"Say something."

"I do not know what to say." Then he belied his words by going on in a dazed voice. "You are pregnant. And you called me. I give thanks to the good God above for this. You had little reason to trust me enough to do so."

"*I don't trust you.*" And she couldn't believe he thought she was stupid enough to after the way he had rejected her.

"Yet you called."

"I had no choice."

"Because you are pregnant." The words came taut across the phone lines.

"Because there are complications. I need to know my baby is going to be okay."

"What is this you are saying? What kind of complications?" His Greek accent was very thick. "You are at risk?"

"That's one way of putting it." And she explained what the doctor had told her, but omitted her recent trip to the emergency room.

Somehow, she didn't think that would go over very well.

He asked a ton of detailed questions, including who her general practitioner was and the name of her obstetrician, in addition to many more questions about her two related conditions that she hadn't thought to ask when she'd been at the doctor's office. It embarrassed her to have to say she didn't know, but he never once accused her of being negligent with her baby's health.

His lack of condemnation did not stem the impatience she felt with herself for being such an ostrich about everything.

When she told him about Dr. Pompella's recommendation for termination, he swore viciously in three languages. She didn't know if it was because the doctor had recommended it or because Rachel had refused to comply.

Having no real desire to find out, she didn't ask.

"Give me your contact information." The abrupt order after all that swearing startled her.

Too unsettled by his unexpected reaction to ask why he wanted both her home and work address as well as every contact number she could be reached at she gave him her details. Even if it did seem like overkill.

"And now, you are all right now?"

"I'm fine." She justified her answer with the thought that they would not have released her from the emergency room if she hadn't been.

"I will talk to you later," he said tersely and rang off.

CHAPTER SEVEN

RACHEL stared at the now dead phone in her hands for several seconds.

The sound of surf came in through her open patio doors and the wicker back of her chair rubbed against her shoulder blades like it always did, but she felt distinctly like she'd stepped out of her own little apartment into an alternate reality. One where Sebastian Kouros was not such a pig.

Their discussion had gone nothing like she'd envisioned it. There had been no recriminations, no charge of entrapment, no denials of parentage, though he had not acknowledged his fatherhood either. Shockingly, he hadn't made a single base accusation, if she discounted his assumption she'd gotten married within three months of giving her virginity to him.

And she couldn't really blame him for that. She had given him a different last name.

As far as she could tell, he had not even been angry, but why had he hung up so abruptly?

Maybe he was trying to decide if he believed her. Perhaps, like her, he needed time to come to terms with what was happening. She hadn't exactly faced up to reality all in one go and for him, it had to be even worse. He'd ditched her and now she came up pregnant, a woman he didn't want, didn't trust and had obviously hoped never to see again.

The other side of her nightmare being pregnant by a man who could be such an arrogant slime.

Only he had not reacted like he was in a nightmare. If she could believe her own ears, she would have to say that the tone of voice she'd heard the most from his end had been relief, closely followed by concern. How could a man who believed she was the lowest of the low be worried about her?

There was black humor in the situation if she allowed herself to see it, but instead of laughing she felt a painful twinge in her heart. She'd been numb emotionally for months and she didn't welcome this sign her feelings might be coming back to torment her. Then she realized in all likelihood it was an actual physical ache caused by her condition.

It had to be. She had nothing left inside her heart to react to him on an emotional level.

Thoughts of Sebastian, the baby and her medical condition whirled around in Rachel's mind like perpetual motion spinners making it impossible for her to sleep that night.

He hadn't called back and she didn't know what that meant. No matter how many times she went back over the phone conversation, she got no closer to unraveling the puzzle of the man who had fathered her child and then rejected her with such devastating cruelty.

Added to that, fear for the future and the health of her unborn baby kept her emotions keyed to nerve-racking levels of tension. She tried to find a comfortable position to sleep, but no matter which way she turned, she could not get her body to relax enough for somnolent rest. Finally, her blankets and sheets in a tangle, she gave up and got out of the bed.

A cup of hot milk always helped in books, so she zapped some in the microwave, added a bit of sugar and vanilla because it sounded good and drank it.

She didn't feel appreciably more tired or relaxed, but she went back to her bedroom, determined to get some rest.

The messy pile of sheets, askew pillows and her royal blue silk comforter attested to her restless night. She would have to remake her bed before she could even think of getting back into it.

She had fluffed her pillows, put them back on the bed and was snapping the top sheet into place when her doorbell rang. A quick glance at the bedside clock told her it was three in the morning. The doorbell pealed again, it's long drawn out sound, insistent on an answer.

The pale blue sheet fluttered from her fingers and she stared at her bedroom doorway, undecided about whether or not to answer that summons. She could not think of anyone who might visit her in the middle of the night. None of her mother's friends had her current address and none of the people she knew would be so discourteous.

The insistent peal came again and irresistibly drawn by the summons, but nervous about what it could mean, she padded along the carpeted hallway to the front door. She stopped in front of it, adrenaline rushing through her, making her heart beat too quickly for comfort.

A fist pounded against the steel door and she pressed a hand against her breastbone, trying to steady her heart rate as she looked through the peephole. At first she saw only a snow white dress shirt, looking less than pristine, undone at the neck and no tie. She couldn't see the man's face, but she would recognize him on her deathbed.

Sebastian.

She flipped the locks, dismissing the adrenaline rush she felt at the surprise at seeing him, then flung the door open.

Her lips parted in order to greet him, but silence issued forth, not sound.

His eyes were dark as slate with unnameable emotion and set in a face that looked almost haggard in its tiredness. He was thinner than the last time she'd seen him, as if he'd been ill recently and stress lines bracketed his mouth. The past three months must have been pretty hairy businesswise for him to look so worn.

Her hand went out toward him in an involuntary bid to confirm the reality of her vision with touch, her mind unable to accept that Sebastian Kouros was actually standing on the other side of her entry.

He reached out and grabbed her hand in his bigger one just as her heart started galloping madly again. Her breath came in short gasps and she prayed she was not about to pass out again.

She didn't get the chance.

He moved with lightning speed to swing her into his arms and carry her back inside. "Where is the bedroom?"

She pointed down the hallway and he carried

her to it, laying her down right on top of the sheet she'd just spread smoothly over the bed. The gentle sway of the waterbed mattress added to her feeling of disorientation.

"Are you all right? Do you need a doctor?"

"No. The shock of seeing you… It… I just got a little breathless, that's all."

He tensed. "I should have called to warn you of my arrival, but I thought of nothing but getting to you from the moment you called."

He couldn't mean it like it sounded, that he had been out of his head with missing her.

"Because of the baby," she surmised, latching onto the real reason for his apparent concern quickly.

He might not accept he was the father, but family loyalty would make him check. Her brain told her there was something wrong with that reasoning, but she was too enervated to figure out what.

His mouth set in a grim line. "That is no doubt what you believe."

"Isn't it the truth?" Nothing was making much sense at the moment.

It was the wee hours of the morning, she was tired and seeing Sebastian always threw her off balance, but even so, the conversation wasn't going in any discernable direction she would have expected.

Just like earlier on the phone.

"I was concerned about our child, yes, but I was concerned also for you."

Remembering how easily he had evicted her from his life and under what circumstances, she shook her head. She was tired, not stupid.

"I find that impossible to believe."

He nodded, his expression bleak. "I knew this would be so."

Bully for him. It didn't take a genius brain to figure out how little he cared for her.

Then something about his statement struck her. "You said *our* child."

"Yes."

"You believe the baby is yours?"

"Yes."

"You don't want tests?" She couldn't take it in.

"There will be no tests."

Air she had not realized she'd trapped in her lungs expelled in a big rush.

His lips twisted in a cynical smile. "You look surprised, *pethi mou*."

"Thoroughly shocked more like."

"Then the rest of what I have to say will no doubt leave you gasping for breath." His gaze roamed over her with undisguised concern. The man really wanted to be a father. "Perhaps it is best left until morning."

"You're leaving?" she gasped, struggling to sit up.

Totally against what she knew to be best for her, she did not want him to go, could not stand the thought of being alone again.

Lowering his big body to the waterbed frame beside her, he pressed back against her shoulders, keeping her in place. "Relax. I am going nowhere."

"But…"

"I will sleep on your couch tonight and we will talk in the morning."

Since her *couch* was a wicker settee that would have left *her* cramped, she couldn't picture it.

"You would be more comfortable in a hotel." She hated saying it, but knew it to be the truth.

He shook his head, his black hair glinting under her bedroom's overhead light. "I do not want you out of my sight again."

"Don't be silly. You can come back in the morning. I'll still be here."

"You are not safe on your own, Rachel." His fingers tightened on her shoulders. "Until you are on the right medications, your health is at risk."

She moved a little and he looked at his hands.

Relaxing his hold on her with a chagrined expression, he said, "I am sorry."

"I can't take medication. The doctor said so." Well, perhaps that was not exactly what Dr. Pompella had said, but everything about the appointment was hazy after Rachel learned she was pregnant.

"The doctor should have her medical license revoked. This is not true." Derision laced his words.

Her fingernails bit into her hands as they curled

into fists. "I won't take anything that puts the baby at risk."

"I would not ask you to."

She calmed down again, disturbed at how good the warmth of his hands on her shoulders felt.

He removed them, standing up. "Perhaps you have some extra bedding for your sofa?"

"You'll never be able to sleep on it." She got up too and retrieved her royal blue silk quilt from where she'd tossed it on the floor earlier.

She finished making her bed, her mind offering a solution that she wondered if she had the courage to offer.

"I will not leave you alone." The fierceness of his tone left her in no doubt he meant what he said. "If that means sleeping on the floor, I will do so."

"I knew you would protect the baby once you realized it was yours." The words slipped out before she thought better of them.

"So, at least you trusted me that much."

She shrugged, supposing he was right. Her belief in his commitment to family *was* a trust of sorts and it hadn't been misplaced…not like her belief in his integrity as a lover.

She sighed and eyed the king size water bed that took up most of her small bedroom. She'd gotten it for a song when two of her neighbors moved in together. It was a small apartment complex on the beach and though she was introverted in many ways, she'd gotten to know most of her neighbors well enough that she'd been offered the bed first off.

It was definitely big enough for her and Sebastian to sleep with an ocean of space between them.

A year ago, she would have been terrified to share a bed with him platonically, afraid she would give away her desire for him in her sleep. She no longer felt anything like that. And after the way he'd booted her from his bed two and a half months ago, she wasn't worried about him taking the invitation the wrong way.

"You can sleep in here."

"I will not allow you to be evicted from your bed." He sounded really pained.

She actually smiled.

It had been a while and her cheeks felt tight from the effort. "I wasn't offering to sleep elsewhere. The bed is a California king. We can both sleep in it all night without touching."

Sebastian said nothing in reply to her false assumption, too dumbfounded that she had offered to share her bed.

"You do not mind me sleeping in here with you?" he asked in amazement.

Her green gaze did not waver. "The sexual side of our relationship is over for both of us, so I'm not worried about you trying to take advantage."

Her words stung his pride. "I did not take advantage before. You were with me all the way."

"Not all the way, Sebastian. I didn't go with you on your nasty minded mental journey that left you convinced I was a living replica of my mother."

No, she had not. He had made that journey all by himself and could blame no one but himself for the results.

Her small bow mouth twisted in a worried frown. "The truth is, I'm afraid."

"Of what are you afraid?"

She yawned, her eyes red with fatigue. "I don't want to faint like I did at work with no one around to make sure the baby is all right."

"You fainted?" He'd practically shouted the words, but she'd told him she was fine.

Her expression perturbed, she bit her lip.

"Tell me the truth, *pethi mou*."

"I'm not a liar, no matter what you'd like to believe," she bristled.

"You told me you were fine." He hadn't meant that to sound like he was accusing her of dishonesty, but her expression told him that was how she'd taken his words.

"I was...am fine. They would not have released me from the hospital if I hadn't been."

"You were in the hospital?" His insides clenched in fury and fear.

She had been ill enough to go to the hospital and he had not even known. He would not contemplate what would have happened if she had not called him to tell him where she was. His investigator would have found her eventually, Hawk was too good at his job to have failed, but success could have come too late.

"It was just the emergency room. My coworkers called the ambulance when I passed out."

He shook his head. They would have to talk about her job tomorrow as well. Working under the current circumstances was insane, but he did not expect her to see that.

"I think it is time we went to bed."

She nodded, smothering another yawn with her hand, a hand that should be wearing his wedding ring. He waited until she got into the bed before turning off the light and joining her. Rachel's breathing smoothed into an even pattern denoting sleep almost immediately.

He had a hard time taking in how easily she had slept. He was too keyed up for sleep. He had ached to see her again, to share her bed and those things had come to pass, but not like he had expected them to.

She had not wanted to see him, but had forced

herself to call for the sake of their unborn child and she had allowed him into her bed only because she believed the sexual side of their relationship was over. He did not agree, but acknowledged it might take him some time to make her see things his way. He had hurt her badly. However, she had been too responsive before his slide into temporary insanity to completely shut him out on a physical level.

If he did not believe that, he would have no hope at all for their future.

He certainly wasn't going to reach her any time soon on a emotional level. She didn't trust him worth a drachma.

Using the passion between them was the only way he could think to bind her to him at present, but he could not employ it yet. Such a move would not be safe for her until she was on the medications the doctor he had consulted told him about and he was determined not to hurt her again.

In any way.

He could and would control his urge to seduce, but he had made no promises not to touch her in the night. She'd made that assertion they could sleep together without touching. He knew that for him, such a thing would not be possible. Not after ten weeks of searching for her only to find her in peril from her health and pregnant with his child.

He waited until she was in deep sleep before gently pulling her into his arms, and allowing himself to slip into much needed sleep with them wrapped tightly around her.

For the second time, Sebastian woke up beside Rachel.

It felt right. He savored her unique scent and the feel of her warm silky skin against his. She slept in an oversize T-shirt which had ridden up so that they were thigh to naked thigh. He'd come to bed in his boxers and been surprised she had not objected at all to his lack of clothing, but then she said she no longer wanted him.

The sex was over for her.

He counted the days before he could challenge that assumption. However, he would not push her tolerance of his presence by allowing her to wake up in their current compromising position.

Her tiny feet were tucked between his calves and his morning erection was pressed against her delectable bottom. It felt incredible, but he did not think she would agree if she were to awaken in such a position. She would accuse him of *taking advantage*. Her comment regarding that the night before still bothered him.

He'd messed up the morning after, but their time together in bed had been perfect and their passion had been mutual. If she had convinced herself otherwise because of what had happened afterward, he had little hope of her giving him another chance.

Carefully, so as not to wake her, he disengaged their bodies and got out of the bed, but he did not immediately leave the room. Bright morning sun filtered through the window shades and he watched her sleep. She was so beautiful. So gentle.

And the mother of his baby.

He gave thanks for her pregnancy, certain that

had she not conceived she would never have contacted him again. And Heaven alone knew when Hawk would have found her otherwise.

He'd engaged the services of the international investigative firm the day she left, but she'd made it out of Greece without leaving even a trail of her flight. Sebastian understood that now. She'd been traveling under a different name. *Newman.*

He could not believe it had never once occurred to him after the rather one-sided discussion with his mother that Rachel might take that sort of concrete action to distance herself from such a notorious woman as Andrea Long Demakis. She'd made a totally new life for herself in the States and had told him that day in the study how much she'd hated the media attention.

He appreciated the reality of how separate her new life was from her old one after trying to find a clue to her whereabouts in Andrea's New York apartment. The only number Andrea had had there for Rachel had been disconnected two years previously.

He'd asked his mother how she'd contacted Rachel to apprise her of Andrea's death. After another lecture on his intelligence, or lack thereof, she had told him the contact information had been in an address book of Andrea's. Rachel had tossed it when cleaning out her mother's things. His mother's attitude had softened toward him when she realized he had no idea of how to contact Rachel, but wanted to.

Later, he had remembered Rachel's claim that one of Andrea's friends had contacted her and he'd had Hawk interview the women known to be in Andrea's circle of cronies. The investigator hit pay dirt when he'd literally had to offer money to one woman for Rachel's E-mail address.

Sebastian had tried to contact her that night only to discover the E-mail account had been de-activated when the message came back to him as undeliverable.

Hawk had been working on tracing the account when Rachel called.

Yes, Sebastian had many reasons to give thanks his woman had gotten pregnant the first time they made love, but he was also concerned about her health. The fact she'd been going along without treatment for two weeks made him want to hit something.

He wasn't a violent man, but damn it...she could have died.

Rachel walked into the kitchen, her nose sniffing appreciatively at the smell of bacon, buttery toast and aromatic coffee.

She stopped on the threshold of the room at the sight of a bowl of freshly prepared fruit in the center of her small Mission style dinette table. Even more shocking was the spectacle of Sebastian standing at the coffeemaker, his feet bare and his dress shirt hanging loose over his lean hips.

"You have hidden depths, Mr. Kouros." She took a deep whiff of the Sumatran blend coffee. Her favorite. "I would never have guessed you for a closet cook."

He turned from where he was pouring coffee into mugs and she realized his shirt was not only untucked, but unbuttoned as well.

Bronze skin rippled over rock hard abs as he leaned over to place one of the mugs on the table. "I am not, but one of my bodyguards is handy in the kitchen. He just left."

From the look of the perfectly prepared breakfast, the bodyguard had been cooking when Sebastian had woken her to tell her she had fifteen minutes to shower.

They ate in silence for a little while before she asked, "Where did your security team stay last night?"

What she *really* wanted to ask was where Sebastian had slept last night? As in, had he slept on her side of the bed with his arms around her? She thought she'd woken up at some point and been surrounded by male warmth. She'd felt protected and slept better than she had since leaving Greece, but he'd gotten out of bed before her. She simply could not be sure it had been a harmless dream, but she much preferred that scenario to her body finding instinctive and unconscious comfort in his presence.

"They stayed in a nearby hotel."

She pulled out one of the ladder-back dinette chairs and sat down. "Nardo was okay with that?"

His security chief made sure the bodyguards followed him everywhere. Although they stayed in the background, there had even been security men in the apartment and at the villa the whole time she'd been there.

"He was not given a choice."

She bet Nardo was an unhappy head of security this morning.

"I don't mean to be a problem for you."

"You are not a problem." He joined her at the table, his coffee mug in one hand, his gaze disturbingly intent on her. "You are the mother of my unborn child."

"You say that with such assurance, but I'm still surprised you didn't want tests." About traumatized by astonishment really.

"You were a virgin when we made love. The baby could have no other father."

"You're sure of that now?"

"Yes."

"For heaven's sake, why?" Nothing had

changed that she could see, but all of a sudden she was not some awful man-eating liar.

What was going on here?

His big shoulders tensed. "You reacted like a total innocent. I should have given that more credence the next morning, but I did not."

"You were too busy making assumptions because there had been no blood." He was so medieval, he should be in a museum.

His gray gaze darkened with some intolerable emotion. "You said you were attacked."

"And you said I was making up stories in order to trap you like my mother had used lies to lure Matthias in." That had hurt so much.

She'd never told anyone about what had happened in her teens and to have the one person she shared it with disbelieve her had been as devastating as his wholesale rejection.

At that moment, granite and his jaw could have competed in the rigidity stakes. "We would do better to forget the things I said the morning after we made love."

Just like that. Amazing. She was having his

baby, so she was supposed to pretend everything was fine between them?

She didn't think so.

CHAPTER EIGHT

"So, ARE you saying you now also trust me about my past?"

"That is what I am saying."

She shook her head, not believing him for a single second. It was too easy, too much of a blanket acceptance of what he had violently rejected before. "I wish I could understand why you are so sure the baby is yours."

She was certain the rest of his supposed newfound faith in her stemmed from that belief.

He looked wary and that pricked her curiosity.

"What changed, Sebastian? When I left your apartment, you thought I was little better than a whore."

"Never that."

"You accused me of using my body for financial gain. What would you call it?"

"Stupidity."

"Tell me why."

He looked distinctly uncomfortable. "My mother thinks I am a fool."

"You're kidding, right?" Greek mothers revered their sons and Phillippa thought Sebastian and Aristide were the best the male species had to offer.

Besides, what did Phillippa's opinion have to do with Sebastian changing his?

"She called me a dinosaur and said that lack of blood is no indication of a sexual past."

It took a second for the meaning of his words to sink in, but when they did, Rachel jumped from her chair and screeched, *"You told your mother about us having sex?"*

What must Phillippa think of her? Here Rachel's mother and stepfather had been less than two weeks dead and she'd been hopping in the sack with Sebastian. It had to have appeared indecent to Sebastian's mother.

Heck, it *had* been indecent.

Sebastian reached out and anchored her wrist. "Sit down and calm yourself, Rachel."

She did sit, but only because she started feeling woozy and didn't want him to realize it. She yanked her wrist from his grasp and glared at him. She'd spent her whole life calm and had never even realized she had a temper until Sebastian started pricking at it after the funeral.

"Please tell me you did not discuss what happened between us with your mother," she gritted out between clenched teeth.

Red scorched Sebastian's cheekbones. "I told her, yes. And I believe it was the first time in my life my mother spoke freely to me about matters of a sexual nature. It would please me if it were also the last."

If she hadn't been so angry and mortified, she would have laughed at his aggrieved expression. The fact he had accepted his mother's opinion on a matter she had no firsthand knowledge of, but not Rachel's personal avowal also rankled.

"So, Phillippa believes I told the truth about

being a virgin and you accepted your mother's opinion as Gospel after pillorying me as a liar."

"That is the way it was, yes."

"Did she tell you she believed me about the other too?"

"No! I did not bring this up to her."

"*Why not?* You told her everything else."

"Not everything." He rubbed his eyes as if tired.

She wondered how much sleep he'd gotten the night before. They'd gone to bed in the wee hours of the morning and he'd woken up before her.

"What, did you forget to mention what color of socks I was wearing?"

"You weren't wearing any socks. Your lovely legs were bare and I did not go into that great a detail with my mother. I would not do such a thing. Have I no credit in your eyes at all that you could believe I would do so?"

Realizing she'd really offended him with that remark, she still shook her head and told him the truth. "No, pretty much not any."

He grimaced. "Well I did not." He waved a hand toward her food. "Eat your breakfast. You need your strength."

For the baby's sake.

Looking down at the beautifully prepared food, she thought he had really jumped headfirst into protective soon-to-be father mode. She mentally shrugged. She would not give daylight to the wish that some of his concern could have been directed toward her person rather than her role as incubator.

That kind of thinking was in the past.

She no longer cared that Sebastian could not love her. She would not let herself.

Without eating any more of the still half-full plate of food, he got up and put it on the counter. Turning to face her, he leaned his tall, hard body against the cupboard.

His silent scrutiny unnerved her and her breath caught in her throat at the partial view she got of his chest because of his open shirtfront. Her gaze slid down of its own volition and she almost choked on that held breath.

His stance outlined semi-aroused male flesh and she felt an unwelcome answering response in the heart of her femininity.

She couldn't possibly be experiencing desire for him.

Not after everything that had happened.

Yanking her gaze from his body, she concentrated on her food.

"When you are finished here, we will go to see a specialist about your thyroid and heart." She could not tell from his tone of voice whether or not he had noticed her appraisal.

She nodded her head, not looking up, not wanting to know.

"While we are gone," he continued, "my people will start packing your things. If there is any furniture to which you have a sentimental attachment, we can have it shipped to Greece or the New York apartment for now."

Her head snapped back and she met his eyes in a hurry on that one. "Packing me? What are you talking about? I'm not going to Greece."

His gorgeous face gave nothing away.

Villains were supposed to be ugly with oily mustaches, like Simon Legree, not men who could compete for the cover of a woman's eye candy magazine.

"Rachel, you need looking after. I cannot do that from half a world away. You will come to Greece."

He was so arrogantly sure he knew what was best and just on principle, she opened her mouth to argue, but then snapped it shut again. Hadn't she called him for this very purpose?

She wanted someone who would take care of her baby if something happened to her. He might be going about it in his usual, King of the World manner, but this time she'd let him get away with it.

"Okay, but we don't have to pack up my apartment. I won't be pregnant forever."

"Yes, we do."

"Why?"

"Your pregnancy may not be permanent, but the changes it will affect in your life will be."

He was right, but she still wasn't going to let

him tell her when it was time to move to a bigger place. "I can get by in a one-bedroom until the baby is old enough to walk at least."

"As my wife you will have no need of this rental or to *get by* with anything."

Her heart started beating too fast and she had no idea if it was the stupid arrhythmia or Sebastian's extraordinary statement offered much too casually.

He'd said it like them marrying was a foregone conclusion, but, "I don't remember being asked if I wanted marry you."

"What you or I want is not important right now. Our baby must be brought into a secure environment of two parents willing and able to care for it."

"I don't have to marry you in order for you to be there for the baby."

"Yes, you do. Anything less than marriage between us will shortchange our child a parent and deprive me of the opportunity to raise him."

"Maybe I don't want to be *shortchanged* by a husband who thinks I'm a good candidate for slut of the year." She pushed her plate away, having eaten more than Sebastian, but not all of it by any stretch.

He crossed his arms over his chest, his expression bleak. "I told you, I do not think this of you."

"Yes, you do. Don't think I'm stupid enough not to see you're only being nice to me for the baby's sake, but that does not change your real opinion of me."

"I told you that I no longer believe you lied to me."

"You don't have to think I'm a good person to believe I was a virgin. For all I know, your Machiavellian brain has come up with some nefarious reason for me giving my virginity to you particularly. I mean, obviously a schemer like me would have purposefully forgotten protection in the hopes of getting pregnant by you and to trap you into supporting me and my decadent lifestyle for the foreseeable future."

"I did not say these things!"

"But for all I know, you're thinking them." She

sighed, feeling tired all at once. "I know how you feel about family, Sebastian. You believe my baby is yours because your mother convinced you I didn't lie about you being my first lover. That means you will do whatever is necessary to protect your unborn child, even pretend a rapprochement with a woman you despise as a manipulative liar."

"You do not trust me at all."

Had he just worked that out? "You know, one thing still leaves me wondering. You've never even raised the possibility of me having gone to bed with someone else in the three months I've been home from Greece. After all, there is no shortage of sexy, available men in Southern California."

Molten fire shot from Sebastian's eyes. "You will go to bed with no other man."

"But how can you be sure I haven't already?"

"You were attacked. You were afraid of intimacy. Although you overcame that fear with me, there is no guarantee you could with another man."

"You've got an incredibly fast mind, Sebastian,

but I still don't believe anything you say." She'd made the mistake of trusting him once, even knowing that to trust someone from his world was stupidity itself.

He'd hurt her so much her heart had been frozen. She would not make that mistake again.

Sebastian's hand slashed the air with angry impatience. "I do not think you are a slut. I know you have never had another man besides me and I was the experienced one. If anyone is to blame for the lack of protection that night, it is me."

Well, that explained a little more of what was motivating him now. He was taking on board the responsibility for her unplanned pregnancy.

She was too honest to let him. "Just because I'd never made love doesn't mean I was ignorant about birth control. I just never thought of it."

"I did not either. I was too far gone."

Was there some significance in his admission? She refused to look for it.

"So, it was both our faults. That does not mean you have to pay the ultimate sacrifice by marrying me."

"This is a wasted discussion. I do not like talking in circles. You are going to marry me and the sooner you accept that, the better it will be for everyone involved."

"You think so?"

"Yes, because you are too smart and too conscientious not to do what is best for both you and our unborn child."

"What do *I* get out of this?" she demanded, incensed that he could truly believe marriage to him would be best for her.

"I will sign the island villa over to you and settle money on you so you will never be without."

"You want to buy my baby?"

He came away from the counter in an explosion of movement and pulled her from her chair to face him. "I do not want to buy *our* baby, nor am I buying you. I am taking care of you. That's all. Okay?"

He sounded really driven, but she couldn't work up enough moisture in her mouth to answer. She'd never seen him lose his cool like this before. Not even that time on the beach when he'd been trying to convince her to stay in Greece, had he been like this. His hold wasn't hurting, but he was just vibrating with fury.

He released her and stepped back. "We'll talk about it later. You have a doctor's appointment."

It turned out she had three doctor appointments and Sebastian insisted on being present for all of them. The thyroid specialist explained that her thyroid was actually just beginning to go into the hyper condition and that she could take medication to control it during her pregnancy at no risk to the baby. The heart specialist explained that the same meds that controlled her thyroid would most likely prevent a flare-up of the atrial fibrillation. And the gynecologist told her that once the beta-blockers kicked in, she could resume natural intercourse without risk to her heart or the baby.

She had not appreciated that particular piece of information, or Sebastian's audacity in asking for it.

Which she told him in no uncertain terms as the limo pulled away from the curb in front of the exclusive clinic Sebastian had taken her to.

"It was a necessary question," he argued, his feelings fully under wraps as if he'd never lost his cool in her kitchen.

"How do you figure that?" She was still feeling belligerent and more than willing to let him see it. "I just could not believe you asked the doctor if it would be safe to resume sexual relations. *We don't have sexual relations.* We had a one-night stand."

"It was not a one-night stand."

"How else would you define it?"

"Anticipation of our wedding vows."

"You're incredible!"

He smiled sardonically. "Thank you."

She huffed out an angry breath and he sighed.

"Face it, Rachel, a platonic marriage between the two of us will be an impossibility."

"First, I have not said I would marry you and second, if I did agree to marriage it would only be with the stipulation we have separate bedrooms."

"No."

Just that. One word. No arguments, no justifications. She couldn't believe he was so arrogant he really believed she would let him touch her after the way he had rejected her. What, did he think she was some kind of masochist?

Well, she wasn't. "I told you, I don't want sex with you again."

Sebastian turned so his body faced her. "Really?"

An aura of danger filled the interior of the limousine and although he hadn't moved any closer to her, she found herself wanting to back away from him.

"Yes, really," she said with a voice that quavered embarrassingly.

"Let's see, shall we?"

"What? No—" But her protest became nothing more than muffled sound against his lips.

He did not demand, he did not force, but used a gentle seduction she found infinitely more difficult to fight. He slanted his mouth over hers again and again with a barely leashed hunger she could sense in the tautness of his body, though his lips were tender on hers.

Her body, frozen for weeks, woke as if it had never been asleep or known bone deep numbness. A million electric impulses jolted through each nerve ending, sending so many messages of pleasure to her brain, she was on instant overload.

She had thought she was detached, but in reality, she had been starved for a sensation only he could give her.

He seemed to sense it and cupping her face in his big hands, he brushed sensually against her jaw with his thumbs. His tongue teased the seam of her lips, seeking permission to enter. She gave it on a low moan, parting her lips in blatant invitation.

He took immediate advantage, sliding his tongue into the warmth of her mouth, tasting her as if he could never get enough of the intimate kiss. She responded with a wantonness that horrified her mind, but her body was powerless to combat. She felt a connection to him that was too primal to be impacted by logic and too strong to be severed by even the still open wounds he'd inflicted on her heart.

"You taste so sweet," he said against her lips and pulled her onto his lap.

She didn't protest, but found herself burrowing into the warmth his body provided, her arms locking around his neck.

He was her anchor in a passionate storm of hurricane proportions.

His hands skimmed over her curves, cupping her breasts and playing with their hard and throbbing peaks through the thin fabric of her bra and oversize silk blouse until she thought she would go mad. She squirmed against him, reveling in the evidence of his desire under her bottom. She wanted his mouth on her and did not protest when he started undoing buttons.

Her bra fastened in front and with a deft flick of his fingers, it was undone. He peeled the fabric back from her swollen flesh and began an exploration that left her breathless and panting from desire.

Suddenly her heart was beating much too fast, feeling like it would pound out of her chest and she could not get enough air into her lungs no matter how hard she tried.

She broke her lips from Sebastian, terror filling her. "Sebastian, stop. I can't…"

His head came up with a snap and he looked at her with passion dark eyes. "What?"

"My heart…" She wheezed, trying to breathe.

He cursed, his eyes filling with concern and a horrible self-directed fury. *"What was I thinking?"* he asked, his accent very thick. "Rachel, are you all right, *agape mou?*"

The sensation began to subside as quickly as it had come upon her and she nodded.

He leaned over, one arm locked securely around her, and pressed the intercom button for the front. He rapped out a series of orders in Greek, then sat back, adjusting her so she was completely surrounded by him and her head was resting on his chest.

"I should not have kissed you yet." His deep voice was laced with remorse. "We have not even filled your prescriptions." He cursed in

Greek again. "I am sorry. I did not intend to put you at risk."

"You had no business kissing me at all." Her anger lost some of its impact in translation seeing as how she was cuddled up against him, her fingers now locked in the smooth fabric of his shirt and feeling too physically weak to move.

"You are my woman. Kissing you is my right."

So much for remorse.

"Except when it puts you at risk. Then I must show self-restraint." He spoke in an undertone as if admonishing himself.

"I may be the mother of your child." She sat up so she could look into his implacable gray gaze. "But I am not your woman."

"You can say this after the way you responded to my kiss?"

"Yes." But fresh out of arguments to support the stark, one-word answer, she let her head fall against his chest again.

The sensation of weakness lingered even though her heart had settled back to a less erratic rhythm. It was still beating too fast, though.

Minutes later, they were back at the heart specialist and Sebastian was berating the world renowned doctor for allowing her to leave his clinic without having given her a dose of the prescribed medication. The man, who was probably one of the most eminent men in his field, stammered an apology and quickly arranged for her to take her first dose of betablocker.

Sebastian was not content and insisted she be kept in the clinic for overnight observation. He would not fly her home to Greece until he was sure she was strong enough to make the trip.

"I am sorry, *yineka mou*. It is my duty to protect you, but I took your health risk too lightly. On the surface, you seemed so healthy, so much like your usual stubborn self, I did not realize how fragile you really are."

She pressed the button to make her bed sit more upright, having given in with bad grace to his insistence on her staying overnight under a doctor's surveillance. She knew it was the right thing to do, but she had not counted on the sense of obligation she would feel toward Sebastian when she'd called him. Everything he did to take care of her made her feel like she was in his debt and she didn't like it at all.

"I'm fine. You heard the doctor. My heart would have to get a lot more stressed before we would have to worry about a heart attack or stroke."

His face turned to stone at the words and she wished she hadn't been so specific. Sebastian's complexion was the color of the ocean on a cloudy day and his slate gray eyes were bleak.

"I am sorry," he said again.

She would be willing to bet that he had apologized more in the last hour than he had in his whole adult life.

While she thought he *should* feel bad for kissing her when he had no right, she felt uncomfortable with his excessive guilt over her *reaction* to the kiss. He believed that by exciting her physically, he had set off her atrial fib when in fact, anything could have caused it.

She bit her lip and watched him, conflicting emotions tearing at her conscience.

"I wasn't doing anything more strenuous than sitting at my desk when I fainted and had to be taken to Emergency."

He looked at her as if his superior brain for once could not make out the meaning of what she was saying.

She spelled it out for him. "I could have had the atrial fib attack even if all I'd been doing was sitting beside you in the car, minding my own business. It was not your fault."

"It was." Sebastian was as terrifying in guilt mode as he was when he was angry.

There was no reasoning with him.

"According to the doctor, within twenty-four hours on the beta-blockers, we don't need to be worried about another attack, even if we make love." She'd blushed the color of a red ball sunset when the heart specialist had felt compelled to share that information, but she hoped reminding him about it would derail Sebastian's guilt trip.

"This is good." His smile was shocking after the past hour of him looking so grim. "I am glad you have reconciled yourself to sharing my bed."

"I haven't," she said, horrified he'd taken her words that way.

"If you have not then why bring up the future safety of such an event?"

"I was trying to get you out of guilt mode," she said with total exasperation.

"Strange that you should care about my emotional well-being when you hate me so much."

"I never said I hated you."

He looked way too complacent at that assurance.

"I said I don't trust you and I don't."

"You trust me to take care of you and our baby."

"That is not the same as trusting you to be my lover again."

"Since you have had no other lovers, I am still your lover."

"Stop arguing semantics. I am not going to bed with you again."

"That is all right. We can make love on the couch like we did the first time, but heed this, Rachel. We will make love again. It is inevitable."

She glared at him. "It is not inevitable."

His smile said she was wrong and she wished she could be a little more certain in her own heart she was right.

Sebastian talked her into staying in the clinic for five days until her blood work showed improvement in both her conditions. Heaven alone knew how he achieved it, but the heart specialist and two EMT workers flew to Greece on Sebastian's private plane with them. When they arrived in Athens, she was given a thorough going-over by the heart specialist before being allowed to make the helicopter trip to the island.

The man was not allowed to go home until he had gone over her medical history with the doctor Sebastian had procured to stay on the island during her pregnancy. She learned from one of the maids that Sebastian had also upgraded the clinic on the island to be equipment ready for most medical emergencies.

Rachel couldn't even begin to imagine the expense he'd gone to in order to make that happen. The man was obsessed, but since knowing medical help was available if she needed it made her feel more secure, she didn't so much as tease him.

Nevertheless, the extensive preparations surprised her when he could have kept her in Athens more conveniently in regard to both his business and her medical care. She was even more shocked when three mornings after her arrival on the island, she woke to live music outside her bedroom window. While she was still reeling from the effects of waking up in such a manner, a knock sounded on her door.

She called out permission to enter, feeling disoriented.

Phillippa came into the room, her lovely face wreathed in smiles. She must have been ferried over early that morning because she had not been on the island the night before when Rachel went to bed.

The older woman went to the window and pulled back the drapes. "It is a beautiful day for a wedding."

Rachel had barely digested that statement when one of the maids arrived carrying yards and yards of white satin. Close behind her came another maid with a shoe box under one arm and a huge bouquet of flowers in the other.

Having said not one word, Rachel sat bolt upright in bed and did what any woman would do when faced with a surprise wedding she had not agreed to. She screamed and then she jumped out of the bed and starting yelling Sebastian's name.

Phillippa and the maids stood stock-still in shock. They no doubt thought she'd lost her mind, but that was no comparison to what they were going to think when she murdered Sebastian. She rushed out of the room, ignoring the cold stone of tile on her feet out in the hall.

"Sebastian Matthias Kouros!"

When he didn't show himself, she stormed down the stairs intent on finding the rat and giving him a piece of her mind.

When she did find him he was leaning against the doorjamb of his study. He looked much too complacent for a man facing murder and mayhem.

She stomped right up to him and shoved her finger in his chest. "How dare you set up a wedding and not tell me? Do you know your mother is in my room right this minute wondering what happened to her future daughter-in-law? She's going to be upset damn it when the wedding doesn't take place."

Sebastian's eyes went over her like seeking hands and the unwelcome flutters in her stomach made her even madder.

"Stop it."

"What?" he asked in a lazy masculine drawl.

"Looking at me."

"But you are so lovely to look at."

With her hair on end and wearing an old T-shirt she'd filched from him one summer a couple of years back when she'd needed something to put over her swimsuit when some of her mother's friends arrived unexpectedly? Not likely.

She glowered at him. "Well, don't do it like that."

"And how am I looking at you?"

"Like you own me." And regardless of her ap-

pearance, the flare of desire in his eyes was un-
mistakable. "Like you want me."

"But these things are true. You belong to me
and I want you more than I have ever wanted
another woman. Do you have any idea how
arousing you are in a temper?"

She wanted to spit nails. "Sebastian!"

"What is it? I do not think this upset can be
good for our baby."

"You should have thought of that before you
started trying to take over my life."

He straightened away from the doorway,
towering over her in all his gorgeous magnifi-
cence. "I do not wish to take over you life. I
wish to share it."

She laughed, feeling and sounding pretty much
hysterical. "You don't want to share my life. You
want to share my baby."

Suddenly strong fingers latched around her
waist and she went airborne until she came up
against unyielding male flesh, her face only
inches from his.

"Let us get one thing straight, Rachel. We are

both parents of that baby inside your womb and I cannot share its life without sharing yours. Do you want to limit my fatherhood to occasional visits and holidays? Is that what this is all about? You want revenge for the way I treated you and you have latched onto the fact that refusing to give our baby my name and refusing me twenty-four, seven access to our child, you will achieve it. But have you considered that your revenge on me will also cause pain for our child?"

"I don't want revenge." She couldn't believe he thought that was what this was about. "I have no intention of withholding our baby from you."

"Then marry me."

"I don't have to marry you for you to be my baby's father." Only for the baby to carry his name, they did have to marry.

She hadn't considered that aspect to the situation, but he had and so would their child one day.

Sebastian released her, setting her away from him.

The expression on his face was unlike anything she'd seen there before. He looked defeated.

"So, you refuse to marry me."

All she had to say was *yes* and she knew as surely as she knew how to balance an account book that if she said it, he would accept her decision and let her go.

She couldn't make herself say the word.

She'd been numb with pain for months, had hidden behind an emotionless wall of self-protection when he kicked her out of his life. But learning of her pregnancy had started the disintegration of that wall and his arrival back in her life had demolished it. He wouldn't let her ignore him and in forcing her to come face-to-face with his role as the father of her child, she had also faced another irrefutable fact.

She still loved him.

She didn't want to, but if his actions the morning after they made love could not kill her love for him, she did not know what would. So she was faced with spending the rest of her life without him, or living with the man she loved, knowing he did not love her. It was an untenable choice and not one she could make on the spur of the moment like this.

The way he had treated her that morning had to be weighed against the gentle way he'd treated her prior to Andrea's death. Also, since coming back into her life in California, he had done his best to be a caring and considerate guy…except his deplorable belief she belonged to him because she was pregnant with his child.

And then there was how he had planned their wedding without her say-so or input. "I don't appreciate having my wedding planned without me even agreeing to get married, or my opinion being taken into account on the arrangements."

"Are you saying you would marry me otherwise?"

"I'm saying I will consider it, but you have to ask me, darn it, and you are not planning my wedding without me."

A wary hope filled his eyes, making him appear vulnerable and doing more to soften her heart than anything he'd done since coming for her in California.

"Then, I will court you."

* * *

Rachel walked back into her bedroom, bemused and a little worried by Sebastian's offer to court her.

Phillippa stood beside the window, her back to the door. The wedding dress, shoes and bouquet were arranged carefully on her bed which had been made. The maids had gone, but the air of expectancy remained and the border-line positive thoughts she'd been entertaining about the overconfident man downstairs fled.

How dare he leave her in a position of having to tell *his* mother there would not be a wedding?

"The music has stopped." Phillippa turned, her expression thoughtful.

"It was a mistake."

"It is Greek tradition to play the music outside the bride's window on the morning of her wedding."

"But there isn't going to be a wedding."

Phillippa's eyes, so like her son's, reflected worry. "Did you and Sebastian argue?"

How could Sebastian have left her to deal with this?

"We never made up to begin with."

"I am sorry to hear that. I had hoped that with a baby on the way, you would find common ground."

He'd told her that too? "Your son has a big mouth."

Phillippa's mouth curved in a surprising smile as she moved away from the window. "Not usually, but I believe with you, he is out of his depth and therefore acts out of character."

Sebastian out of his depth? Not likely. "Your son is more sophisticated than I could ever hope to be."

"But you do not hope this, is that not true? You have no desire to pursue the lifestyle your mother sought after so wholeheartedly."

"I prefer a quieter existence."

"And Sebastian has very little experience with a woman uninterested in the jet-set lifestyle. He knows nothing of women who possess such innocence and integrity."

"He does not believe I have integrity."

Phillippa shook her lovely head. "You are wrong, I think."

"He thought I lied to him about… About…" She couldn't make herself say it, but Phillippa already knew anyway as her next words confirmed.

"He regrets doubting you in that."

"Only because *you* told him he was wrong."

"A man does not take his mother's advice unless he wants to, Rachel," Phillippa said wryly.

"If you say so." Her gaze kept slipping to the wedding dress on the bed and finally she went over and touched the sleek satin folds.

Sebastian had spared no expense. Rachel might not shop top designers, but no daughter of Andrea Long Demakis could reach adulthood without recognizing them.

"Sebastian was engaged once before."

The comment so shocked Rachel that her head snapped 'round so she could meet Phillippa's eyes. "He was?"

"Yes. To a woman much like Andrea."

Rachel's stomach began to churn. Would she never live down her mother's image?

Phillippa reached out and squeezed Rachel's

arm. "I see the best parts of your mother in you, child. You do not share her weaknesses."

"Sebastian thinks I do." And maybe he was right.

After all, she could not control her desire for him even when she had every reason to despise him.

"Nonsense, but he finds trust difficult. The woman in his past burned him very badly and then Andrea came on the scene. She destroyed a man Sebastian loved like a father and my son's cynicism toward women cemented into rock-like certainty. It was very difficult to watch, but I could do nothing to stop it."

"He had you as an example." Rachel wasn't nearly so understanding about Sebastian's pessimism. It had hurt her too much. "He has to know that not all women are manipulative, status seeking, gold diggers."

"*Ne,* yes…he had me. However, he was very young when his father died and he does not remember much of my marriage. He knows only that I came from a simple fishing village and married a man twenty years my senior, a man wealthy enough to buy my village and everything in it."

"He couldn't possibly believe you married his father for money." It was unthinkable.

"I do not know, but he has few memories to combat his current view of women. My husband, though I loved him very much, was not a demonstrative man. He worked long hours and our age difference meant that we shared few friends or common interests."

"Yet you loved him."

"Just as you love my son despite the fact your own lives are so different."

She wasn't touching that one, not even in a Hazmat suit…it was a concept much too hazardous to her peace of mind.

Phillippa sighed at her silence. "Although my son's view of women was jaundiced, I had thought he saw something different when he looked at you. He was always careful of you, so concerned for your welfare when you were younger."

"Until Andrea and Matthias died. Then he hated me." She remembered the inferences he'd made in the study the day the will was read. "It was as if when she died, he transferred his dislike of my mother to me." And it had hurt unbearably.

"He was grieving." Phillippa shook her head sadly. "My son does not express his emotions easily. You were the scapegoat for his pain and I am sorry to say I did not see it until too late."

"It wasn't your fault."

The other woman's air of guilt did not diminish. "I tried to play matchmaker, leaving the two of you alone together on the island, hoping privacy and proximity would accomplish a fond mother's dreams."

"You did that on purpose?" Rachel should have realized, but Sebastian wasn't the only one who had been struggling to come to terms with someone's death.

And she would never have expected Matthias's niece to think Andrea's daughter was a worthy candidate for wife to her son. The Demakis and Kouros families had every reason to want to be rid of Long women permanently.

"Yes, but my plans backfired."

"I'm sorry." She hated to see Phillippa looking and sounding so defeated.

She was a truly kind person and a very caring mother. That counted for a lot in Rachel's book.

"No, it is I who am sorry. You were hurt through no fault of your own. Sebastian was too emotionally volatile after the funeral to make good relationship choices. I should have known this. I am his mother, but I ignored any trepidations because I did not see how I could throw you two together again. If you went back to the States, I knew you would never return to Greece. You had already made it very clear you wanted a life far removed from that of your mother's. I erred in judgment badly and now you will not even consider marriage to my son."

"It wasn't your error in judgment that caused the problems between Sebastian and me. It was his."

"But I explained that."

"Even if what you say is true and Sebastian's behavior was spurred by grief." And she wasn't sure she bought that scenario. "I'm not about to marry a man who sets the wedding up without my consent and didn't even let me pick out my own wedding dress."

The older woman touched it, much as Rachel had done, running her hands along the soft fabric. "It is a beautiful dress."

"That's not the point."

"He did not ask you?"

"He told me and that's not the same thing at all."

Phillippa's head was averted as she picked up the flowers and smelled them. "Some women might find that romantic."

"If they were loved, maybe. I found it incredibly arrogant."

"So, you will deny him his place by your side because he knows his own mind and acts on it?" For the first time, Phillippa's voice echoed with censure toward Rachel and she faced her with a frown.

"He's going to court me." She didn't know why she'd said it, maybe because she hated to see this woman she admired so much disappointed in her.

Phillippa's expression cleared and a relieved

smile creased her features. "Ah, that is a good thing. He should have thought of that to begin with."

Yes, he should have, but the truth was a man didn't automatically think to court a woman he was marrying solely for the sake of their unborn child.

Sebastian's intended courtship had a rocky start when he called Rachel into his study later that afternoon so she could sign papers to receive ownership of the island villa. His accountant was also in attendance with information on her new money market account, checkbook and a slew of credit cards in her name. Sebastian wanted her taken care of in every way he could devise.

Not that his efforts on her behalf had done any good.

Her response to his offer of the villa had been anything but positive.

"I don't want your money, or your house." She pushed the papers away, refusing to sign them, her green eyes dark with anger.

Why should she be angry he wanted to give her a home?

"You should have inherited more than the book collection when Matthias died, but I was too angry after the funeral to appreciate that fact. This only makes things right."

"Matthias was my mother's husband, not my father. He owed me nothing."

"I am your child's father. You cannot say I owe you nothing." He mentally dared her to deny his pronouncement.

She glared her defiance at him and did just that. *"You owe me nothing."*

"This is not true."

She jumped up from her chair and paced across the room, stopping in front of a shelf filled with framed photographs of his family. All of the ones with Andrea's image had been removed. He had seen to it.

Now he wondered if he should have left at least one for Rachel's sake.

"I am not my mother. When are you going to realize that fact?" She spoke with her ramrod straight back to him, her beautiful chestnut hair up in a twist, revealing the vulnerable column of her neck.

He wanted to walk over there, take her in his arms and press biting kisses on the spot he had discovered was an instant erogenous zone for her.

"I did not say you were."

She spun around, ignoring the other two occupants of the study as if they were not there. "Then why give me the house? You don't have to buy access to your child. I already told you that. *I would never do to our baby what was done to me.*"

She vibrated with anger and something else, a vulnerability he did not want witnessed by others. He dismissed his men, including the security guard outside the door, leaving him alone with Rachel.

"What do you mean, *what was done to you?*"

Her expression turned haunted, her bow-shaped lips going bloodless as she bit them. "My mother took me away from my father when I was a small child. I never saw him again and when I got older she refused to tell me who he was so I could find him."

Andrea Demakis had been a bitch of the first order. "What of your birth record?"

"I don't know where it is. She refused to give it to me or tell me where I was born."

"You could have hired a detective agency."

She laughed, the sound more bitter and hollow than anything he'd ever heard from her. "That kind of investigation costs thousands and I don't have anywhere near your kind of money, Sebastian."

He considered that. If what she said was true, and he was past the point where he doubted her on the principle she was anything like her mother, then it was another nail in the coffin of his stupidity three months before. "But you want to know your father?"

"Yes. I remember him loving me."

The words slammed into Sebastian like a powerful anvil. For all that Andrea had done to his family, she had done infinitely worse to her daughter. No one could ever have accused the self-centered woman of loving anybody, least of all the sensitive woman before him.

"Yet, he did not seek you out." He could have bitten his own tongue out after speaking.

Damn it, she did not need a reminder that neither of her parents had cared enough about her to see to her best interests.

"No. I believe he tried, but I think Andrea made it impossible. I remember being so sure as a little girl that he would come for me, positive that my daddy would never forget me. That kind of trust was not instinctive to me. He had to have earned it."

Sebastian wondered. She could be right, or the man could have been more like her mother than Rachel wanted to believe. He would find her father and determine for himself if reuniting with the man would hurt or heal his woman.

"Is this why you are so opposed to me taking care of you? Andrea taught you not to rely on anyone."

"I'm not against it. Not for now anyway. I don't really have a choice, do I?" Rachel crossed her arms over her chest as if protecting herself and it made him furious she felt the need to do so with him, but it was obvious she did.

And he knew also it was his own fault.

"Once the baby is born, I can go back to work, but I wouldn't have called you if I wasn't going to accept your help in the interim."

The fact she had trusted him to stand by his responsibilities was little consolation at the moment. "You called me solely because you feared for our baby's welfare."

"Yes."

Her confirmation gutted him, but he gritted his teeth against saying anything. She had good reason not to want to see him again otherwise, but no matter what he had said, he could not fathom her believing he would permanently let her go after what they had shared.

"And would I have ever found out about my child if you had not become ill?"

"I told you, I would not have kept your child a secret from you once it was born. Both of you deserved a chance to know each other."

He should be grateful for at least that much, but

he wasn't. He wanted far more than grudging duty from the woman standing before him, looking so beautiful she made him ache with wanting her.

"Yet you would have gone through pregnancy alone because you did not trust me to be there for you."

He could see the truth in her beautiful green eyes. Given the choice, she would have kept *him* out of *her* life completely, even if she had allowed him access to their child. The only difference now was her health and as much as it pained him, he had to be grateful for it.

"I'm not alone now," she pointed out, as if comforting him.

He was not in the mood to be comforted.

First she had refused to marry him and now she wanted to refuse everything else he offered her. "Nor are you without financial resources if you would but accept them."

"I didn't get pregnant in order to extort money and houses out of you." Her eyes flashed disdain at him.

"I never thought you did."

She remained silent and he sighed. Okay, so at one time he would have accused her of such a thing, but that time was past. Could she not see it?

Grabbing the back of his neck with one hand, he thought how best to put what was in his mind.

This sort of talk was not something he enjoyed. "When you come to my bed, I want it to be of your own volition."

"What?"

"I do not want you to marry me, or accept me back into your arms because you feel you have no other choice." It was a matter of pride that she take him for himself, not his money.

His attempt at an explanation had done no good.

If anything, she looked more offended. "I wouldn't do that. I value myself too much to trade my body for security."

Why was she so stubbornly refusing to understand?

"Once you own the villa and have sufficient funds, the issue will not arise."

"*I don't want them.*"

"You are being foolishly stubborn."

"And you are not going to get away with trying to buy a place in my bed."

Did she not realize that was exactly what he did not want to do? Apparently not, because she left the room ten minutes later, not having signed the papers and refusing even a checkbook with her name on it.

His first attempt at courtship had flopped.

Rachel snuck into the small sunroom off the kitchen and slipped onto the window seat, curling her legs under her. The room was unused most of the time; the family preferred to eat together in the spacious dining room. It was empty now and that's exactly the way she'd wanted it.

She needed a break from Sebastian's brand of courtship. The man didn't know the meaning of the word restraint. Dozens of roses filled her room. Boxes with jewelry she refused to wear resided in the top drawer of her dresser and he spent lots and lots of time with her, feeding her need for him, but not assuaging her fear one iota that he did it all for the baby's sake and not her own.

If she could convince herself that even one half of what he was doing was for her and not merely to ensure his role in the life of the baby she carried, she would have been in heaven. As it was, she struggled to stay out of a hell of uncertainties about his feelings and his lack of trust in her basic integrity, despite what he said to the contrary.

He gave lip service to trusting her, but he never stopped trying to cajole her into taking the villa. She refused on the principle that if he truly believed she were not like Andrea, he would trust her to make the decision about marriage irrespective of financial gain even if her current financial state was less than exemplary.

And she desperately needed him to believe she was nothing like Andrea.

"I thought I would find you in here."

Her heart quickened like it always did when he was around, but the scary arrhythmic beat had not returned since she went on the beta-blockers.

"I was going to read for a while." She lifted the paperback she'd carried with her into the room for him to see.

His dark brow lifted. "You would rather read in a little used room of the house than on the beach when you love to be outside?"

"It's quiet in here."

"You were hiding."

She blushed guiltily. "I wanted to be by myself for a while. You said you had work to do this morning."

"The morning is over and I cannot help but notice you bolted for your hole at the same time I said I would be done."

Frustrated that her plan to spend time alone regrouping her defenses had been so quickly foiled and feeling inexplicably defensive, she frowned at him. "You don't have to spend all your time with me. It's not required for your *courtship*."

"No doubt you would prefer I left you alone entirely. Now that your health is assured, you are content to pretend I do not exist."

As if that were possible. "I—"

"You will rejoice to hear that I must return to Athens on business," he said mockingly, interrupting her midword.

"When do you leave?"

"In an hour's time. Were I to invite you to come along, I am sure it would be wasted breath. You heart is a stone where I am concerned."

Man, he was in full-throttle pessimism mode.

"That's not true."

"Is it not? You refuse my gifts and avoid me at every opportunity."

"One attempt to find some privacy is hardly avoiding you at every opportunity." She remained mum on the gifts issue because to his way of thinking, he was right.

She refused to be bought.

"Do not let me interrupt you." He indicated her book with a scornful sweep of his hand. "You have far more important things to do than to spend your time conversing with me."

The truth was, she wouldn't mind some time on her own, but she'd never seen Sebastian like this. He seemed almost hurt.

She opened her mouth to speak, but he forestalled her again.

"Maybe the time away will accomplish what my presence has not." He turned to go.

She could not stop herself from reaching a hand out to him. "Sebastian."

He shrugged off her hold. "Do not concern yourself. I am leaving Nardo. He will make sure you have all that you need."

A week later, Sebastian had not returned. He had called each day, but their conversation was stilted. He asked about her health and she asked about his business. Neither topic required a great deal of discussion. She was feeling great and his business problems were dragging on.

No matter how good the managers, some negotiations required Sebastian's touch. Or at least that's what she tried to tell herself, but in the dark of the night she tormented herself with thoughts that Sebastian was using his business as an excuse to be away from her.

A man used to being fawned over by the most beautiful women in the world wasn't going to take easily to her cold treatment of him. She'd been so angry with him when he brought her back to Greece, hating everything he did for her that made her feel indebted to him.

He was right. She'd refused his gifts, his overtures, all of it, because she hadn't trusted him. He'd hurt her and she could not believe he wanted her for herself and not their child, but did that mean she should continue to withhold herself from him?

Was being married for the sake of a child the worst thing that could happen to a woman? Wouldn't having to learn to live without the man she loved be even worse? Or having to stand by and watch him marry one of those gorgeous sophisticates he had dated before her. The thought sent a chill down her spine.

Although she'd tried to block Sebastian from her life completely, she'd had a morbid need to read the European tabloids during the three months she'd been in California. Not once had he been featured with a new woman. It was like Sebastian Kouros had dropped off the face of the social scene entirely. And that had been her single consolation in their being apart.

She told herself that he was as alone as she was.

But really, she had no reason to believe that. He

could have had a more discreet relationship with a woman. Maybe that woman was even now in Athens pacifying his ego bruised by Rachel's inability to forgive and forget. She wished she knew how to simply let the past go, but she couldn't.

After her childhood and near-rape at sixteen, she had trusted no one, men especially. Then she'd met Sebastian and he had been kind to her. She had trusted him on an instinctive level she'd never understood, but he had betrayed her trust, rejected her love and accused her of being the one thing she'd determined never to be.

A carbon copy of Andrea Long Demakis.

Even though she still loved him, she didn't know how to let herself be with him. She was scared of being hurt again because she could not turn off her feelings with him. She'd learned to do that with Andrea, but Sebastian got to Rachel on a level her mother had not even striven for.

She flipped onto her back, the dark shadows in her room no comfort from her thoughts. Why was love so hard for her? Andrea, who had never loved a single person in her life, had been loved by many, but Rachel had been loved by no one except a father she'd been torn away from.

The phone rang, shrilly interrupting her gloomy thoughts.

She rolled over to eye the clock. Midnight. Who would be calling so late? Could something have happened to Sebastian?

She clambered across the bed to reach the phone on the table. She pushed the button. "Hello?"

Another voice said something in Greek at the same time.

Then Sebastian spoke in Greek and the other extension clicked, leaving her alone on the line with him.

"Sebastian?"

"It is I."

"Are you all right?"

A low, bitter laugh came across the line. "Do not tell me you care. I am nothing to you now."

"You're the father of my child. That's hardly *nothing*."

"The sperm donor, you mean."

"What a crazy thing to say."

"It is not crazy to know I can mean nothing to you if you will not marry me."

She settled against the headboard in the darkness of her room. "Getting married will not solve our problems."

In fact, it was bound to create more since their emotional commitment would be so far divergent.

"It will solve my problems. I will be able to take you to my bed again. I will no longer spend my nights aching with a need I have no right to sate."

"You haven't even kissed me since coming back to Greece." And it had worried her.

What kind of courtship included not close physical contact? The kind where a man was trying to convince a woman he didn't really want to marry him, that's what kind.

She realized she'd said the words aloud when a furious Greek curse assaulted her ears. "You think I do not want you?"

Then he went off in a barrage of Greek, none of which made any sense to her. She spoke very little of the language and none of the words he was saying.

"Did I not show you in California how much I still wanted you? I put your health at risk because I could not keep my hands from your body, my lips from your mouth."

"Well, I'm fine now and you're doing an admirable job of keeping them to yourself."

"I did not wish to dishonor you again before marriage."

"A simple kiss is hardly going to dishonor me," she said sarcastically.

Really, he'd have to come up with something better than that to convince her he was interested in her as a woman.

"The lovemaking that would inevitably follow any kiss between the two of us would."

"A kiss doesn't have to end in sex."

"It does when a man wants a woman as much as I want you."

"Are you saying you physically desire me, but you won't take me again until we're married?"

That was ridiculous. He hadn't minded making

love to her before when they weren't married and he'd made sure she knew he was making no promises of commitment either.

"Take you, *yineka mou?* You have a very primitive view of our lovemaking."

Her feelings for him *were* primitive. Primal even. And they went too deep for her to ever extricate them from her being.

"You know what I mean."

"I believe I do and you are correct. The next time our bodies join, you will be my wife in name as well as spirit."

"What do you mean *as well as spirit?* I'm not your wife now. You had me without commitment the first time and you made sure I knew it."

"I had decided to marry you by the time I was inside you."

He couldn't be serious.

"That's not what you said the next morning."

"I went crazy the next morning. I drew conclusions. I said things that should not have been said, but none of it changes the fact I married you in my heart when I made your body one with mine."

If he spoke the truth and he had no reason to lie, he'd made a *huge* commitment to her that night. She hadn't asked him for one, but the depth of his reaction to their lovemaking explained the strength of his response to his own twisted logic the following morning. He'd been as gutted by his conclusions as she had been.

"How much longer will you be in Athens?" she asked, incapable of responding to his claims, but moved by them all the same.

He sighed. "I do not know."

Her heart sank. "Oh."

"You sound disappointed."

"I am."

A pregnant silence greeted her honesty.

"It doesn't mat—"

He didn't let her finish the lie. "You could come to the apartment."

The invitation shocked her, even though it shouldn't have.

"Of course you would not wish to come," he said before she could even open her mouth to speak. "What am I thinking?"

"You're wrong," she slotted in before he could go off on another one of his negative assumption scenarios.

"You wish to come?" he asked, sounding more shocked than she'd felt at the invitation.

No amount of time on her own was going to shore up her defenses against him and it *hurt* to be away from him.

Taking a deep breath, she let it out in a whoosh and then said, "Yes."

"The helicopter will arrive in the morning."

"I'll be ready."

She was, even though the helicopter arrived shortly after daybreak. Nerves made the flight to Athens seem short and the pilot was landing all too soon on the roof of the Kouros Industries building.

Sebastian was there, helping her climb out of the helicopter. He pulled her away from the still rotating blades, keeping her body close to his own and tucked down in a protective way. Once they were clear, he stopped.

His mouth covered hers before she could say

anything and his lips tasted so good, she didn't want to.

Strong arms closed around her, pressing her into the already aroused contours of his hard male body and he kissed her with soul searing intensity.

Her lips clung to his as he pulled away and she melted against him with the first sense of rightness she'd had in months. Tipping her head back, she looked at him, drinking in his appearance with thirsty eyes.

His were bloodshot, but fixed on her with intensity that belied their tiredness. "You came."

"I said I would," she reminded him breathlessly, her lips still tingling from his kisses.

"So you did."

"Your helicopter came early."

"I hoped you would be ready."

"I was."

The conversation was inane, but the undercurrents were explosive. What neither said, but both felt as exhibited by their actions was a desperate need to be together as soon as possible.

"Are you also ready to marry me?"

She swallowed. "You go right for the jugular."

He shook his head. "It should be smooth, romantic, but I am not feeling smooth. I need you to say you know you are mine."

She could see that he did and to deny him was to deny herself.

Not strong enough to deny them both, she said, "Yes."

The kiss that followed her acquiescence completely overwhelmed her so that she was not aware of being picked up and only became conscious of her surroundings when a shocked gasp accompanied her and Sebastian's exit from the elevator he had carried her to. He lifted his head as her eyes opened and she got the distinct impression from the chagrined expression on his face that it was a wholly new experience for him to be caught necking in the elevator by one of his employees.

The gasp had come from an older woman manning the desk in the lobby. She stared at the president of her company as if he'd grown two heads and started talking in Swahili.

His jaw taut, Sebastian nodded to the receptionist and carried Rachel right out of the building to a waiting limousine.

They were inside, her sitting on his lap, a very noticeable bump under her hip, when he spoke again. "When will you marry me?"

"As soon as you like."

"Do you want a big wedding?"

She smiled her approval at his desire to know her desires and not just assume they matched his own. "No."

"Do you want to be married on the island?"

"It doesn't matter."

She'd long ago learned that the trappings of life did not make a bit of difference to the underlying circumstances. She'd never dreamed of a princess style wedding, she'd only ever hoped she got to marry the prince.

And she was going to.

Sometimes he acted like a frog, but that wasn't so bad. At least he knew how to apologize and he listened. It might take her screaming into his face, but he could be persuaded to look at an alternative perspective. After all, he'd canceled his planned wedding and agreed to a courtship because she'd wanted it. His flexibility gave her hope for the future.

That flexibility was not much in evidence when Rachel said she wanted Phillippa at the wedding and Sebastian told her his mother was traveling and would not be back in Greece for a week.

"I cannot wait another week to take you to my bed," he said.

Heat pooled in a place she didn't even want to think about. "You don't have to."

"Yes, I do." His grim look did not suggest he was open to discussion on the subject. "I will not dishonor you again."

She glared at him, but none of her arguments swayed him. It was either marry now and share a bed, or marry later and him go to stay in the company apartment because he did not trust his libido in the same home with her.

They were at an impasse.

The last week had been one of the most miserable of Rachel's life. She'd missed Sebastian in every fiber of her being. She didn't want to spend another week living in his apartment while he lived elsewhere, but she wouldn't tell Sebastian that and admit her weakness to him either.

And it only got worse when he took the decision right out of her hands. Back in full guilt mode, he refused to have the wedding until his mother could be there because it was important to Rachel. He berated himself for pushing her and informed her that he could control himself for a week to assure her happiness with the wedding plans.

He didn't remind her that if she'd agreed to the original wedding, his mother would have been in attendance and they would be living together now, but Rachel latched onto that truth at lightening speed all on her own. She insisted on wearing the dress he had picked out for her, appalled when she realized he was going to dump it in favor of letting her pick out her own gown. She'd loved the dress, just not the way he'd steamrolled over her without a thought to what she wanted.

She sat on the sofa they had made love on the first time late that night, nursing a mug of warm milk and unable to sleep. Sebastian's all-out determination to make her happy scared her spitless. If she allowed herself to believe it was personal, she was afraid she would be setting herself up for disappointment. Yet it felt really personal.

It didn't feel like the consideration of a man who only wanted her to agree to marriage for the sake of their unborn child.

Of course there was the sex thing. He wanted her and there was no hiding from the fact. However, could lust, even rampant lust, explain his actions? Wouldn't a man being controlled by needy hormones go for the early wedding and to heck with Phillippa being there?

That week dragged by despite Sebastian's obvious efforts to keep her entertained, but his mood was precarious at best, the effect of having to deny his desire having obvious impact.

By the time she met him at the altar of the old Orthodox church to say their vows, she was shaking with nerves. Although they had made love before, she was nowhere near certain she could appease the voracious hunger she saw in his gaze whenever he looked at her now.

There was a quality to it that had not been there before, a need that went beyond the physical. It was that quality that made her so nervous. Added to her growing hope that he cared for her, her emotions were a mess.

But when she looked into his slate gray eyes for the first time in front of the priest, her fears faded to nothing under the warmth blazing from them. He might not love her, but he *did* care and she loved him. Now and forever.

Their marriage would be what they made of it and she was determined to make the best of the opportunity God had given her to live out her dearest dream.

And it felt like a dream as Sebastian took her to a five star hotel on the outskirts of Athens.

He carried her over the threshold of their room and she smiled up at him, all the love she felt shining in her eyes, if he but knew it.

His breath caught and then his lips slanted over hers with tender mastery.

When he lifted his head, she was dizzy with longing.

"Thank you." His voice was husky with the need reflected in his dark gaze.

"For what?" she asked, confused.

"For marrying me. I promise you, I will make you happy, *yineka mou*."

"Being with you makes me happy," she said on a burst of honesty, her heart too full to keep all of her emotion in.

She couldn't understand what he muttered as his mouth lowered again, but she understood the all consuming fire in his kiss, because the same blaze burned hotly inside her.

They were moving and then she felt the comfortable firmness of a bed under her. The kiss continued with searing heat while his hand peeled her dress away from her shoulder and he touched her. Caressing the slope of her shoulder, he then gently trailed his fingers along her collarbone. The pressure of his lips changed subtly with each touch, the quality of the kiss becoming gentler, more tender.

The first time they had made love, everything had happened so fast, but he wasn't rushing anything now. Sebastian's fingertips explored every centimeter of her exposed skin, her neck, her chest above the swell of her breasts, behind her ears, along her spine, across her shoulder blades. She shivered from the light caresses, her body trembling with powerful emotion.

His tongue had not breached the defense of her lips and he had touched none of the erogenous zones she had expected. Yet Rachel was writhing under him, tears of intense passion leaking out the edges of her tightly closed eyelids.

His mouth broke from hers, his lips traveling up her face to softly sip the moisture from her eyes.

"Why are you crying?" he asked.

"It's so beautiful, I can't help it."

"Yes."

The ready affirmation and lack of worry in his voice when he first asked the question, brought her eyelids open and she beheld a sight so shocking, her body stilled beneath his. Sebastian's eyes were wet too, their gray irises heated to molten metal.

"You are so beautiful, *yineka mou*. And you are mine."

She swallowed, unable to speak past the lump in her throat, but she nodded.

He peeled her dress down farther, exposing swollen curves, flushed from arousal and tipped by hard points that ached for his attention.

"So beautiful," he whispered again as his mouth brushed across the sensitive flesh, his heated breath an erotic caress.

He said the words again in Greek just before taking one turgid peak into his mouth.

She arched up toward him, her fingers locking in his hair, demanding silently that he keep doing what he was doing.

He played with her nipple with his teeth and tongue, teasing her until the sensations arrowing to the core of her being were so strong, she felt on the verge of climax.

"Oh, Sebastian. Please…." Her breath caught as he began to suckle flesh extra-sensitive from her pregnancy. "My darling, oh, yes. It feels so good."

Her tears turned to sobbing gasps for breath while her body bowed and twisted beneath him. The tension inside her tightened in an ever-winding spiral beyond anything she had ever known, even in his arms. Her other nipple strained against a light brush from his fingertip. He stroked it, kneading and caressing the resilient flesh around it until she thought she would die from the pleasure, or explode.

She did both, experiencing what the French called a little death. A monsoon of tidal wave proportions crashed inside her, tightening her body until every muscle was tense, her womb contracting around the baby just beginning to show its presence in her body. She screamed her throat raw, her body locked in an agony of pleasure, her heart exploding with love.

She couldn't stand one more second of the intense pleasure. It was too much, but she couldn't stop crying out enough to say so. And then her body gave a huge, convulsive shudder and went limp against the bed, her mind conscious only on a very hazy level.

She accepted his mouth moving against her lips, but could not make her own respond. She felt small kisses all over her face. Then he moved down her neck, over her chest and to her breasts as he praised her passion, her beauty, and her uniqueness in a mixture of English and Greek.

He rolled away from her and she felt bereft at the loss of his body's warmth.

With energy she had not thought she had, she opened her eyes and sat up. "Where are you going?"

He was taking his clothes off. "Nowhere. I need to make you mine completely, to consummate our marriage with the joining of our bodies."

She didn't know how she would handle it. She was already spent with pleasure, but she nodded. "Yes."

The extent of his arousal and the level of self-control he was exhibiting became evident as the last bit of his clothing fell away. He was more than impressive in his arousal, he was downright daunting. They'd done this before, but she couldn't help swallowing in attempt to bring moisture to a dry throat. Had be been that big before?

Something of her trepidation must have shown in her eyes because he came down on one knee beside her, his hand gently cupping her cheek. "I won't hurt you, little one. I will never hurt you again."

It sounded like a vow and she took it as such.

She licked her lips and then turned to press her mouth into his palm in a sign of trust.

His big body shuddered at the contact. "Will you touch me?" he asked in a voice that she did not recognize.

It sounded so needy and her proud Greek needed no one.

She reached out and tentatively brushed her fingers down the velvet length of him. He moved against her hand, the veins on his erect flesh pulsating with need he made no effort to conceal. It gave her a sense of power. This overwhelmingly masculine guy wanted her so much he was shaking with it.

She curled her fingers around his hot flesh and squeezed.

He groaned. "That's right. *Agape mou,* your touch is perfect."

He'd called her his love again. It must be a sex thing, but she liked it. She caressed him with her hand, marveling at how new it all felt even though they'd spent an entire passion filled night together.

There was something infinitely distinctive about this experience, but she was too caught up in her desire to figure out what.

"I need you, Rachel."

She smiled a secret woman's smile to herself. "Then have me, Sebastian, my love."

If he could use such words during sex, so could she. It might be the only time she would ever reveal the depth of her feeling to him.

He stilled in the act of pressing her backward, his gaze so intense it made her shiver. "Am I?"

"What?"

"Am I your love?" he growled, no pretense of patience or tolerant lover present.

Her mouth opened, her lips working, but no sound came out. She could not admit the truth, but she could not make herself lie either.

His face spasmed with pain. "Of course I am not, but you married me and for that I must be grateful."

"Do you want to be my beloved?" she croaked, her voice cracked from both excitement and strain.

Wariness filled his expression. "What husband does not wish to be loved by his wife?"

One who had married her for the sake of passion and their unborn child?

Only, it was apparent that he *did* want her to love him. Maybe his pride balked at being a means to an end as much as hers did. If she thought it was his heart involved, she didn't know what she would do. Expire from happiness maybe.

However, it was far more likely his pride talking. He had been adamant she not marry him because she had no other alternative. Had fought to get her to take property and money to guarantee such an eventuality could not come to pass. She'd refused and he'd married her anyway, but perhaps this was another side to his insecurity in that area.

One thing became crystal clear as they hung suspended between making love and talking about it: what she felt for him was not limited to his feelings for her. It never had been.

Love was a generous emotion with a need to be expressed, not hidden. If he wanted her love, she would give it to him and they would both feel better because of it.

"I love you, Sebastian."

What he said in response was indecipherable in the swirling vortex of passion he took her to after she said the words.

He finished undressing her with fingers, whose trembling clumsiness made her heart squeeze in response. He touched her all over again, pleasuring her with words and actions so tender she started to cry again. When his hand trespassed between her thighs, she was swollen and ready for him. He touched her until she was crying out with her desire and then he joined their bodies, setting a rhythm that brought them to a mutual, soul altering climax within minutes.

Afterward, he rolled onto his back, taking her with him, so they stayed connected intimately. It was an odd sensation, but incredibly special. She lay, making patterns on his shoulder with her fingertip, loving the feel of his hard muscles under her hands.

"Tell me about the assault when you were younger."

Of all the words she'd expected to hear in the drowsy aftermath of passion, those were not the ones.

She lifted her head from its comfy spot on his sweat dampened chest and looked at him. "Why?"

"I shut you down the morning after we made love because I'd gone crazy with my own assumptions. After I realized how wrong I was, I was haunted by what you'd said."

"So now you want me to tell you about it?"

"Yes, but if it is too painful to talk about, I understand."

A sensitive Sebastian was an unknown

quantity. Even before the untimely death of his uncle, Sebastian had been kind to her, but not sensitive. He'd brought his women around, breaking her youthful heart while repairing it with a smile and a compliment.

"But why do you want to know?"

He looked uncomfortable, but very, very serious. "I never want to do anything that might inadvertently remind you of him."

The words shocked her, but his reasoning touched her deeply. "Nothing you could *ever* do would remind me of him, even if you touched me in exactly the same way."

And she knew it was true, because with Sebastian, everything was different. Her love made it so.

"I am glad."

She took a deep breath, ugly memories playing at the edge of her consciousness. "I've never told anyone but Andrea."

He grimaced. "Knowing her, she was not sympathetic."

That was a major understatement of her

mother's cold reaction to Rachel's trauma. That's when she lost all love for her mother. "She told me to keep quiet about it afterward, never to bring it up again."

"I am sorry for that, *yineka mou*. She did not protect you like a mother should protect her daughter."

She never had.

"No, she didn't." Then Rachel started to tell him.

It had been the night of one of her mother's parties. Rachel had been hiding in her bedroom as usual, trying to ignore what was happening in the rest of the apartment.

A man came into the room and shut the door. He switched on her light and she recognized him as the younger brother of her mother's current lover. He made her feel dirty when he looked at her because he noticed parts of her body her innocent sixteen-year-old mind knew he wasn't supposed to. He was drunk. She could smell the liquor from across the room.

It scared her.

When he sat down on her bed, it scared her even more. He talked to her in the slurring tones drunks use. She told him to leave, but he just laughed and started touching her, telling her she was just like her mother. She screamed and he slapped her. No one in the apartment heard because the music was too loud. She fought, but he got her panties off and his hand was between her legs. He roughly shoved his fingers inside her and she felt a tearing pain that made her scream again.

This time longer and louder than any sound she'd ever made.

The door to her room crashed open and his brother rushed inside. He grabbed the younger man and punched him, calling him names and telling him what a lowlife bastard he was. Her mother came in to see what the ruckus was because her boyfriend's voice had carried where Rachel's hadn't.

When she took in the scene before her, she told her boyfriend to get his brother out of the apartment. Rachel had been sobbing uncontrollably, still hurting between her legs, blood all over her thighs from her ripped hymen.

"Andrea refused to take me to the hospital, saying lots of women bled her first time. But it wasn't my first time. We hadn't had sex and the blood terrified me."

Sebastian's hands were soothing her back although there was tension in his body beneath hers.

"Did you press charges?"

"No. Andrea told me not to say anything, got a lock for my bedroom door and that was the end of it. She married your uncle six months later and we moved to Greece."

"And she appropriated your experience as part of the lure she used to trap him in her net."

"Yes."

The knowledge Sebastian had accused her of doing the same thing shimmered between them.

Grief reflected in the depths of his gray eyes. "I am more sorry than I can ever say for the accusations I made the morning after we made love the first time." The words came out stilted, the English heavily accented with his Greek intonation. "I will understand if you can never forgive me."

She felt a blessed freedom having told him about her past and release from its power in his ready acceptance and apology. "I do forgive you. You were mixed up and said things you didn't mean."

For the first time, she appreciated just how true that was. He really hadn't meant any of what he said that morning. If he had, even his mother's championship of Rachel would not have changed his mind.

He nodded. "To my sorrow, yes. If it is any consolation, I paid for my arrogance. I wanted you and I could not find you. I thought my heart had been shredded."

His heart?

"You looked for me?"

"Yes. But Hawk could find no trace of Rachel Long."

"Who is Hawk?"

"A man who runs an international detective agency. He rarely fails, but you left no trace."

"It's hard to find someone who does not exist."

"You do exist."

"But Rachel Long doesn't."

"This is true. However, I am very grateful that Rachel Kouros now shares my bed, my life, and my future."

"I love you." It was easier to say this time.

His eyes closed as if on an intolerable pain, but when they opened they glowed with warmth that took the very breath from her body. "You are nothing like your mother."

"I know." But she was glad he did too, finally.

"I am very proud you will be the mother of my child."

"Children." She smiled at him, feeling dreamy and full of hope for the future. "I want at least three. I've always wanted a real family."

She'd never liked being an only child.

He shook his head, his expression as grave as she had ever seen it. "Perhaps if we adopt, but you will not be pregnant again."

"What? Why not?" Didn't he want her to have more of his babies? The bubble of happiness around her was starting to lose some of its air.

"It is not safe. This time your pregnancy made your thyroid and heart go out of kilter, next time there is no telling what will happen. No, you must never again become pregnant. I have taken steps to ensure this."

Her head was whirling. He really did have a penchant for drawing crazy conclusions.

"What steps?"

"I am scheduled for a vasectomy in a month's time."

She sat up in total shock, causing their bodies to move in intimate harmony and he groaned. "You can't do that!"

His hands settled on her hips and he arched upward, his semi-erect flesh making itself felt more fully inside her. "I can, *agape mou*. So can you."

They weren't talking about the same thing, but it took her a few seconds of wallowing in the pleasure of his touch to get the breath to say so. "No, I mean, have a vasectomy. That's not necessary. The doctor said I would be fine once we do the procedure after the baby is born. Another pregnancy won't be a problem."

His eyes burned into hers. "I won't risk it."

He'd called her his love and she was finally starting to see that was exactly what he had meant. "You mean you don't want to risk *me*."

"Naturally not." Using his hold on her hips, he moved her in a rhythm that sent her thoughts scattering. "What do you think I am saying here?"

"You love me." Her eyes filled with tears and her heart expanded to fill with a joy she had never known.

He stilled his movements, his hands reaching up to cup her face. "Can you doubt it?"

"But that stuff you said…"

"I told you. I went crazy." The skin across his cheekbones darkened. "You scared me. I felt for you things I felt with no other woman and I did not want these feelings. They were too powerful."

"So, you rejected me." The memory still hurt, but not as much as before.

Because she now realized he had been as devastated as she was by all that had transpired after they made love. The fact it had all been his own darn fault didn't mitigate the pain he'd suffered because of it.

"I rejected my own idiotic image of you, not you." For the second time that night, she saw his eyes glisten with unexpected moisture. "I destroyed something beautiful."

She pressed her hand over his heart. "You damaged it, but you didn't destroy it because we're back together."

"And you still love me?" He sounded uncertain and that shocked her, but she didn't hesitate to reassure him.

"I fell in love with you when I was seventeen and I haven't stopped loving you since. You are the only man I have ever wanted to share my body with, the only one I ever will."

He brought her mouth down to his. "I do not deserve you, but I will never let you go."

"Just you see that you don't." She moved experimentally on him, feeling his body tense under her. "I never want to leave you."

"*S'agapo,* Rachel. I love you more than life."

Talking stopped as she learned a new and

exciting way to make love to him. He allowed her to bring them both to the brink of rapture with her movements before taking over, thrusting up into her, causing an explosion of starbursts to go off in her head while her body contracted around him in love-filled pleasure.

Later, they shared a bath in the en suite's spa tub. Sebastian arranged her in front of him, his hands gently stroking along her curves in a poor attempt at washing her.

"I can't help but notice certain bits are getting very clean," she said with a laugh, feeling light-headed with happiness.

The sense of belonging to someone and knowing they belonged to her was incredible and she laughed again with the sheer delight of it.

His arms tightened around her in unexpected strength. "I would give all that I have to hear you laugh like that many times over the years to come."

"All I want is your love."

"That you will have, *yineka mou*. Every day of my life."

But he gave her more, so much more.

Sebastian showed his love for her in a hundred different ways, not least of which was the difficulty with which she convinced him not to have a vasectomy. It was such a drastic step for the proud Greek man to take, proving to her in a way that could not be disputed just how precious she was to him.

But she wanted more of his babies and it was only after speaking with three specialists, his mother and Rachel arguing until she was hoarse that he finally agreed to one more pregnancy. He did it with the caveat that if there were even minor complications, they would not try it again.

She knew there wouldn't be. She planned to pop out lots of little Kouros babies to love.

A month before their baby was due, Sebastian surprised her with a visit from an American. The handsome, older man with sad brown eyes turned out to be her father and his gaze filled with both elation and warmth when he saw her.

He'd spent the last eighteen years searching for

her, but Andrea had changed their names and done a very good job of hiding from him. She'd taken Rachel out of spite when he had told her he wanted a divorce.

He'd never remarried because he hadn't been able to forget the daughter he'd loved so much.

That night, she lay in bed beside Sebastian, her mind at peace, her heart full. "He'll make a terrific grandfather. He's a wonderful man."

"He has a wonderful daughter."

"Can you believe he's been looking for me so long? He spent thousands and thousands of dollars to try to find me over the years."

"I find that easy to believe. I would never have stopped looking either."

She smiled and brought his hand to rest over her swollen tummy. "Our baby brought us back together."

A month later when the baby was born, their family circle was complete. Her father and Sebastian's mother discovered they had more in common than being the grandparents to a beautiful baby girl and were married the day Rachel discovered she was pregnant with her second child.

Rachel marveled that a life which could be so devoid of love could now be filled with it and she never took for granted the gift she'd found in Sebastian Kouros. He said she was the gift and did everything in his power to make her know how valuable she was to him.

The day she told him she was pregnant with their second child, they both acknowledged that love was the real gift and it kept on giving, filling their lives with the richness only it could bring.